THE FORTUNES OF TEXAS

Follow the lives and loves of a complex family with a rich history and deep ties in the Lone Star State

FORTUNE'S HIDDEN TREASURES

A new branch of the Fortune family heads to idyllic Emerald Ridge to solve a decades-long mystery that died with their parents, and a mysterious loss that upends their lives. Little do they know that their hearts will never be the same!

FORTUNE'S UNEXPECTED GIFT

His entire life, single dad and architect Sander Fortune has put his sprawling family first. So when sparks fly with his cooking class instructor, he falls suddenly—and fast. But when he discovers Lisa Bergen's mission in life is to become a mom, is this a recipe for disaster... or a second chance to expand his circle of love?

Dear Reader,

With the holidays approaching, it's time to get into the giving spirit—whether that's physical gift items, the gift of time or the gift of joy. And while everyone is racing around trying to find that perfect *something* for their perfect *someone*, often it's the intangibles that are best and most needed. A smile, a thoughtful gesture, understanding. When things get tough, the support of those around us helps us get through difficult times and makes us realize what matters most in life.

Sander Fortune and Lisa Bergen are both in need of love and compassion from those around them. He's looking for space and freedom after raising his daughter, his siblings and his housekeeper's son. She's looking for the joy of a child after miscarriage and needs a miracle to make it happen. On paper, they shouldn't be a match. Yet we all know when it comes to matters of the heart, love can be found in the most unlikely places.

In Emerald Ridge, Texas, miracles happen during the holiday season. You just have to know where to look. Get ready to celebrate as Lisa tries to help Sander find his Christmas spirit. Watch Sander fall hard for Lisa, even as he claims that his dreams and hers don't match. Celebrate the joys of Hanukkah and Christmas with family. And don't forget, while parents have a lot of lessons to teach, they never know when their children will teach them the most important lesson of all.

So grab a cup of cocoa and your warmest, coziest blanket and enjoy this opposites-attract romance. I hope you enjoy Lisa and Sander's story!

Jennifer Wilck

FORTUNE'S UNEXPECTED GIFT

JENNIFER WILCK

Harlequin

THE FORTUNES OF TEXAS

If you purchased this book without a cover you should be aware that this book is stolen property. It was reported as "unsold and destroyed" to the publisher, and neither the author nor the publisher has received any payment for this "stripped book."

MIX
Paper | Supporting responsible forestry
FSC® C021394

Special thanks and acknowledgment are given to Jennifer Wilck for her contribution to The Fortunes of Texas: Fortune's Hidden Treasures miniseries.

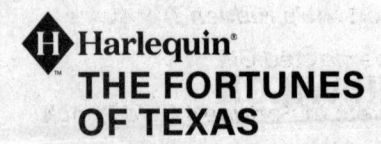

Harlequin
THE FORTUNES OF TEXAS

ISBN-13: 978-1-335-14329-7

Fortune's Unexpected Gift

Copyright © 2025 by Harlequin Enterprises ULC

Recycling programs for this product may not exist in your area.

All rights reserved. No part of this book may be used or reproduced in any manner whatsoever without written permission.

Without limiting the author's and publisher's exclusive rights, any unauthorized use of this publication to train generative artificial intelligence (AI) technologies is expressly prohibited.

This is a work of fiction. Names, characters, places and incidents are either the product of the author's imagination or are used fictitiously. Any resemblance to actual persons, living or dead, businesses, companies, events or locales is entirely coincidental.

For questions and comments about the quality of this book, please contact us at CustomerService@Harlequin.com.

TM and ® are trademarks of Harlequin Enterprises ULC.

Harlequin Enterprises ULC
22 Adelaide St. West, 41st Floor
Toronto, Ontario M5H 4E3, Canada
www.Harlequin.com

HarperCollins Publishers
Macken House, 39/40 Mayor Street Upper,
Dublin 1, D01 C9W8, Ireland
www.HarperCollins.com

Printed in Lithuania

Jennifer Wilck is an award-winning contemporary romance author for readers who are passionate about love, laughter and happily-ever-after. Known for writing both Jewish and non-Jewish romances, she features damaged heroes, sassy and independent heroines, witty banter, yummy food and hot chemistry in her books. She believes humor is the only way to get through the day and does not believe in sharing her chocolate. You can find her at www.jenniferwilck.com.

Books by Jennifer Wilck

The Fortunes of Texas: Fortune's Hidden Treasures

Fortune's Unexpected Gift

The Fortunes of Texas: Secrets of Fortune's Gold Ranch

A Fortune with Benefits

The Fortunes of Texas: Fortune's Secret Children

Fortune's Holiday Surprise

Harlequin Special Edition

Holidays, Heart and Chutzpah

Home for the Challah Days
Matzah Ball Blues
Deadlines, Donuts & Dreidels

Visit the Author Profile page
at Harlequin.com for more titles.

To romance readers everywhere:
Find your joy wherever you can.
And remember, love is in the little things.

Chapter One

Lisa Bergen pushed blindly on the doors leading outside of the Emerald Ridge Fertility Center, oblivious to the cool December breeze or the Christmas decorations adorning the building. Turning left, she wandered into the local park and sank onto a bench next to the playground. She covered her face with her hands and rested her elbows on her knees, trying to process everything she'd been told during her appointment.

A single cycle of IVF cost around fifteen thousand dollars, and the fertility center recommended committing to six cycles. Ninety thousand dollars on a teacher's salary? She only made a modest income as a middle school teacher, a job she loved for the fulfillment it gave her, not the financial perks. She couldn't afford the commitment, even if she delved into the money her husband had left her when he died.

Having a child had always been her dream, ever since she was a little girl. No matter what other dreams she'd had back then—traveling the world, exploring abandoned castles, flying airplanes—every single one of them included her being a mom.

The tears that had welled as she exited the clinic

overflowed and ran down her cheeks as the last of her pregnancy dreams slipped away like a tumbleweed in a barren desert.

She shook her head. No, she wasn't going to fall apart. Not here in the middle of town, where everyone she knew—and even more of those she didn't—could see her. Wiping her eyes, she pulled a pair of large sunglasses out of her bag, even though it was cloudy. Glancing up, she watched what seemed like every female in the state of Texas pushing a stroller with a baby, or a toddler on a swing, and her heart ached. Why couldn't that be her?

She and Jordan had dreamed of having a houseful of children. Lisa released a quavering breath. She'd practically heard the patter of little feet, the giggles of tiny voices, the hushed "I love yous" before bed, whenever they talked about the family they'd one day have.

Unable to stay where she was, she racewalked to her red Subaru Legacy. Once inside the car, she dissolved into a fresh wave of tears. Her therapist, the one she'd engaged after her husband died, had told her it wasn't healthy to keep her grief bottled up. But, while definitely cathartic, crying still didn't ease her sorrow. How was she supposed to exist in a world without a child of her own to love?

Maybe she didn't need to commit to six cycles. Maybe she could do only one. It would still be expensive, but at least it would be something she could afford. Except what if it didn't work? She and Jordan had tried to get pregnant and it had been a lot harder than they'd originally anticipated. Sure, in the beginning, they'd joked about how much fun it was to try, but they'd both gotten discouraged the longer it took. And now, at thirty-eight, the likelihood of her getting pregnant after only one round wasn't realistic.

She pounded her fists on the steering wheel until they ached as badly as her chest. Several minutes later, her tears finally dried. Removing her sunglasses, she looked at her reflection in the rearview mirror. Her amber eyes, rimmed with red from her tears, had darkened to brown in her sadness, and the whites were a scary shade of pink, thanks to her crying jag.

Lovely. Not how she wanted to look for the challah-baking class she was leading at the rec center in—she glanced at her watch—twenty-five minutes. She exhaled. No matter how riotous her emotions, she had to get them under control. She reached for her leather bag in the passenger seat, pulled out her phone, and dialed a familiar number. Her best friend picked up almost immediately.

"Talk me off the cliff," Lisa begged.

"You're afraid of heights, and the wind is going to make your hair frizz," Melissa said.

Despite her sadness, Lisa laughed. She could always count on her snarky BFF to brighten her mood.

"There you go," Melissa murmured. "What happened?"

"I can't afford IVF."

"Oh, honey, I'm sorry. I know how badly you want this."

Lisa swallowed. "No, no, no. Don't give me sympathy. I have to teach a class in twenty-two minutes, and I can't show up as a walking puddle."

"Skip it, and let's go grab an ice cream."

Chocolate ice cream solved almost every problem, but sadly it would have to wait till later. "I can't skip it," Lisa said. "I love teaching the class. Besides, Molly and Olivia are going to be there."

"Those nieces of yours are adorable."

"I know." She didn't mean to wail, but a little one slipped out.

"What about adoption?" Melissa suggested gently.

Along with her dreams of having children had been her desire to be pregnant. As a child, she'd stared at pregnant women in awe. As an adult, she'd wanted to join their exclusive club. When she'd met and fallen in love with Jordan, he'd been just as eager for a family as she was, and they'd gotten started "trying" right away. No one had prepared her for how hard it could be, and when she'd finally conceived after years of trying, the two of them had been ecstatic. Until he'd died of a heart attack right after they found out the test was positive, and she miscarried a month later.

She'd lost her last tie to him, and the devastation had almost killed her.

Four years later she was finally ready to try to have a baby on her own. But adoption?

"I hadn't really considered it," she said. Images of all the pregnant mothers she'd seen recently played through her head. As long as she ended up with a baby, did it really matter how that baby got to her?

"Well, maybe it's time you do," Melissa encouraged her.

"I don't know." She sighed. "I always pictured myself pregnant." Then again, she'd pictured herself with Jordan, spending their old age together too.

"Sometimes we have to change the picture, Lis." Her friend's voice was gentle.

"I know you're right. I'm just…tired of being forced to change my dreams, you know? I know it's selfish, but—"

Melissa scoffed. "It's *not* selfish, it's resilient. You want something, so do whatever you have to do—within legal boundaries—to get your wish."

Her friend was right. Another pregnant woman walked by Lisa's parked car. *Seriously, were they everywhere?*

"Do you have any idea how many of my students' moms are pregnant? I thought middle school parents were past that." She shook her head. Some of her students' parents were her age. She wasn't past it, why did they have to be?

"Oh, honey, I wish things were different for you."

Lisa sighed. She did too. She blew out a breath, making her brown hair ruffle. "Me too." She cleared her throat. "Okay, no more pity party."

"Wait a minute, we didn't even get to the ice cream yet!" Melissa cried.

Lisa laughed. "Why do I like you again?"

"Because you're stuck with me."

"True." They'd been friends for as long as Lisa could remember. Melissa had shared every milestone with her—high school prom, graduations, weddings… Jordan's funeral. She wouldn't have survived without her. Even if they didn't live near each other, she couldn't imagine her life without her best friend.

"You sure you're okay?" Melissa asked, all traces of teasing gone from her voice.

Lisa looked at the clock on her dashboard. "Yes. I've got ten minutes to get myself to the rec center for my class, so I'd better be. But really, I am. Thank you."

"Call me later," Melissa said.

"I will. Love ya."

"Love ya more!"

As she was about to pull away from the curb, the door to one of the nearby offices opened, and Naomi Katz knocked on her car window. Lisa rolled it down.

"Hey, Lisa, I saw you sitting here." Her gaze missed nothing, and Lisa's face flushed. "Are you okay?"

Lisa's heart squeezed, touched by the concern of this woman who didn't know her well, but still checked on her, simply because she looked distressed. People like Naomi were one of the reasons why she'd stayed in this town, instead of moving back to Dallas after Jordan died.

"Oh, thanks so much. Yeah, I'm okay. Or I will be."

Naomi looked a little skeptical. *Great, probably means my eyes are still red.* But Naomi nodded, gave a small wave, and returned to her office.

Blinking, Lisa backed her car out of the parking space and drove to the rec center to prep for her class. No matter what else happened, she'd feel better afterward. The sticky dough, the yeasty smells, the satisfaction of a perfectly braided challah. Baking always made her feel better.

* * *

Sander Fortune shut the front door of his daughter Kelsey's new home and exhaled with relief. He loved her with all his heart. More than that, if something like that were possible. He valued his bond with her more than anything else in his life. Seeing her finally moving into a home with her fiancé, Trevor Porter, and the triplets, happy and satisfied, filled him with pride. He couldn't wait for them to get married. But wow, triplets were exhausting. Thank goodness he was done with all that. A tiny bit of relief surged as he realized he finally had his home all to himself

Memories of raising Kelsey on his own as a single dad, and a few years later adding in his nieces and nephews when his brother and sister-in-law died, assailed him. The chaos, the fear, the loneliness. And of course, the fun. Because it had also been a blast. Despite all the trauma, they'd had a blast together, and the main house was always filled with love. But there'd been little, if any, alone time.

Forty-four years old and *finally* done with raising kids. He took another deep breath, letting the joy of independence slide through him. The new experience of playing with Kelsey and Trevor's triplets was wonderful, but he loved leaving the responsibility that came with raising them to the two of them just as much. Being a grandpa was going to suit him just fine.

If only he had someone to share this next stage of his life with. Because the truth was, sometimes, he was lonely.

He paused, his step hitching on the way back to his

truck, and shook his head. Kelsey's matchmaking attempts must be messing with his brain. Now that she was happy and engaged, she was hell-bent on trying to make him happy, too, getting him "out there," as she said. Like her plans for him today.

"Dad, you have to get out there and get busy," she'd said.

"Busy? I'm plenty busy. I've got my business and my family. How busy do you want me to be?"

She'd shaken her head. "You need to socialize more. With people your *own* age."

"I have friends." He did, good ones that he didn't see often enough. Because unlike him, they were still raising their own families, and finding time to hang out with a friend wasn't high on their list.

Since then, she'd made it her personal mission to recruit him for every activity she could think of where he might meet single women his age. Last week, she'd signed him up for pickleball lessons. He'd scoffed, telling her only old people played pickleball. Except when he arrived at the rec center for his lesson, everyone playing was younger than him. And much to his surprise, he'd enjoyed himself. He'd even gone out for frozen yogurt afterward with the three other people who'd also been taking a lesson along with him. Between debating what flavor to order and sitting around laughing at their escapades with the sport, they'd somehow all agreed to play together again, and now every Thursday at four he had a pickleball date. He shook his head.

Kelsey had been thrilled, but still she hadn't let up, and today's adventure was a challah-baking class he was scheduled to take in less than half an hour. He could have argued or refused to go, but he was a sucker for making his daughter happy. Sander couldn't say no to her, even if he wasn't entirely sure what challah was. When he'd mentioned that, she'd immediately sent him a photo of braided bread. He'd shrugged. He liked bread, even if the only kind he knew came from the store. He'd get to eat it in the end, though, so how bad could it be?

He hadn't told her yet that this was going to be the last class he let her sign him up for. After all, he was a big boy and could meet people on his own when and how he wanted to. He didn't need help making friends, and he certainly wasn't looking for a relationship, no matter how much Kelsey hinted at it. Relationships required him to put the other person first, and frankly, he'd spent his entire life putting others first. He didn't begrudge them, but he was tired.

Sander drove through Emerald Ridge to the rec center, parked his truck, and walked inside, jingling his keys in his hand. Holiday music piped from speakers and he hummed along with it. He hoped challah tasted good. His stomach rumbled. It was a baking class, so maybe they'd put something on the challah, like cheese or roast beef? His mouth watered when he thought about it.

Once past the lobby, decorated in silver and white for the season, he followed the signs to one of the community kitchens, entered the room, and stopped short. The woman at the front of the room, dressed in a blue-and-white apron with Happy Hanukkah and Let's Get

Lit written across it, made his heart pound against his ribs. He stood stock-still, drinking in her tall, lush figure, her long dark hair, and her amber eyes that snapped with joy as she stood, hands on hips, chattering with two young girls. Her luscious curls bounced as she nodded her head and then reached down to embrace the two of them. His mind spun, barely retaining a coherent thought before moving on to something else. There were kids in this class? He'd thought it was for adults. Maybe the two little girls were hers. The instructor looked to be around his age, although he couldn't say for sure. She wasn't wearing a wedding ring, but she could be a single mom. Or maybe she decided not to wear it to bake. Desire for this unknown woman shot through him, sending a trickle of sweat down his spine.

He never reacted this way to women. He didn't believe in instalove or instalust or whatever people were calling it these days. But she definitely sparked his interest.

She glanced his way as he approached, a broad smile on her face highlighting her high cheekbones and white teeth, the front one slightly crooked. "Hi, I'm Lisa Bergen. You're here for challah baking, I presume?"

Her smoky voice drew him forward, reminding him of whiskey and campfires and velvet. A weird combination, but somehow, exactly right.

He removed his hat and grasped her outstretched hand. "Yes, ma'am, I am. Not that I have any idea what challah is, but my daughter signed me up and told me I'd love it."

"It's braided bread, a little sweet and eggy, and your

daughter is right." She craned her neck and glanced behind him. "Is she here?"

He shook his head. "Nope, she's busy with her triplets. It's just me."

A fleeting shadow crossed her face, making him wonder what he'd said to upset her, but it passed just as quickly. "Wow, triplets. That must be fun. Glad to have you."

"Auntie Lisa, Auntie Lisa, Auntie Lisa, when are we making challah?" One of the little girls ran over to Lisa and hugged her waist.

The woman smiled, her cheeks turning a pretty shade of pink as she patted the little girl on her back.

"Molly, go back to your sister, we'll start in just a minute." She turned back to Sander. "I think that was my signal to get this class started. Why don't you find a worktable?"

Would it be wrong of him to take the closest one to her?

"Your daughter seems very excited," he said as he walked with her toward an empty table at the front of the class. "I can't wait."

Lisa shook her head. "Oh, Molly and her sister, Olivia, are my nieces. And my biggest fans." With that, she returned to the front of the room and faced the class.

Sander's heart thunked a little harder. So she was their aunt. That change in status made her suddenly more approachable. *Desirable*. Possibilities cycled through his mind. Was she single? He remembered her lack of wedding ring and hoped she hadn't removed it for this class. His thoughts jumbled as he tried to follow her instructions for making the dough, the sticky concoction adhering to his fingers just as much as she clung to his thoughts. He'd never been a teacher's favorite, yet today, right now, he wanted to be hers. Kind of hard, though, when he was elbow deep in dough and there were lots of other bakers in the class. The last thing he wanted to do was call out a desperate, "Look at me? Is this okay? Will you go out with me?"

He clenched his jaw, just to be doubly sure that none of those questions escaped his lips.

"Okay, everyone, place your dough in one of the baggies on your table. You'll take that home to rise, braid it, let it rise again, and bake it. In the meantime, I'm going to pass out dough that's already risen, so you can learn to divide it and braid it here."

Her hips swayed as she distributed the already prepared dough to the participants. When she reached his table, she smiled and handed him a bowl. Was there something special in that smile just for him? A gleam the others hadn't noticed? Their fingers met as she passed the dough to him, and a spark of heat traveled up his arm.

He really was losing it. "Thanks," he said, his voice huskier than normal. Was it his imagination, or had her head jerked at the contact?

In front of the rest of the class, she demonstrated how to divide their dough into four equal pieces and roll it out into long strips. He followed her instructions, but somehow, his long strips were unequal lengths and skinny in parts and fat in others. And the dough, once separated, didn't smush back together easily. Sander sighed. Maybe it tasted better than it looked. It was a good thing he was an architect and not a ranch hand. His skills lay in the planning, rather than the doing, unlike some of his rancher cousins. He winced. If they could see him now.

Frowning, he tried once again to make four equal strips and gave up almost as quickly when the dough fought him. With a growl, he lined them up on his work surface and tried to remember the braiding instructions Lisa had given him.

"Pinch them together at the top. Start with the left strand and go over, under, over."

He looked up, startled at her presence by his side and then tongue-tied by her magnetism.

She nodded, eyes sparkling. "Go on, you can do it."

"You've got way more confidence in my skills than I do, considering how lopsided these strips are."

She bit her lip, but her silent laughter spilled from her expression.

"Hmph, no fair laughing at your students," he said.

"Oh, I'm not laughing at all my students," she replied. "Just one."

He huffed. "Great way to make an impression."

"I wouldn't worry too much." She looked at him, her amber eyes…admired him?

Heat curled around his neck. Holy hell, he hadn't blushed like this since he was in high school. He studied the challah he was braiding. Definitely wasn't going to win any beauty pageants with its odd bulges and lopsided ends. Unlike Lisa, whose beauty and warmth took his breath away.

"Here, let me help," she said, moving next to him and trying to reshape the challah into something resembling a bread loaf. He thought it was a lost cause, but with her standing this close, and her vanilla scent wafting around them both, he was loath to assert his independence. All too soon, her flurry of hand movements paused, and she stepped back.

"That's not too bad," she said. "And it will taste delicious. All you'll need is a little practice."

She winked at him before moving on to the other students in his class. He blew out a breath and ran a hand through his hair. Then frowned. He'd let it grow longer than usual, to where the ends hit his collar, and he had to tuck the front behind his ear. He'd never much thought about his appearance before, but suddenly he wondered what Lisa thought.

And then he wondered why he cared.

Must be all the newly in love people he was hanging out with, like Roth, Priscilla, Harris, and Kelsey. They, like so many other happily coupled folks, wanted everyone else to experience the bliss they felt. Well, he was perfectly fine on his own and too tired to think of starting over now.

Except every time Lisa's voice carried across the room, something thrummed in his chest. Each time he spotted her out of the corner of his eye, he forgot to look at his dough and instead, stared at her. Despite the yeasty aroma of fresh dough, all he could smell was her vanilla scent. He groaned.

"That doesn't sound good," Lisa said, walking over to him. "I can't have you leaving my class unhappy."

He blinked, realizing that everyone except her nieces had left the classroom.

"Then go out with me." The invitation popped out and surprised him as much as it did her.

She tilted her head to the side, her lips curved in a smile. "So, you're asking me on a pity date?"

He winced. "That came out wrong."

"You're not asking me out, then?" She bit her lip, her shoulders shaking with suppressed laughter.

Running his hands along the rim of his Stetson, he shut his eyes for a moment. *Get a grip, Sander.*

"Lisa, would you like to go out to dinner with me? I'd love to get to know you better."

After a brief moment of hesitation filtered through her beautiful amber eyes, she nodded. "I'd like that very much."

Relief washed over him. "Don't worry, I won't cook," he said, pointing to his lopsided challah. "Instead, I'd like to take you to Captain's."

She gaped at him. "That's awfully fancy for a first date. Are you sure you wouldn't prefer something a little more casual? I'm a sucker for pizza and beer."

A desire to make a good impression poked his conscience, and suddenly the thought of dressing up for a real dinner, with cloth napkins and fancy silverware, appealed to him.

"I'm sure. I'd like to take you to a nice place. However, I'll remember the pizza and beer for next time."

Holy cow, they hadn't even gone out on a first date and he was already planning their second?

Her sparkling gaze penetrated his once again. *Probably wondering how to manage his crazy.* But after all his insecurities that had surfaced during the class, all of a sudden, he didn't mind her attention. He let her stare. Nerves skittered along his spine as he wondered if she'd take him up on his offer. Yet beneath those nerves, there was a sense of calm, something he couldn't explain. Finally, as if coming to some conclusion he hoped was positive, her posture relaxed. "Sounds perfect."

And finally, he let himself smile. "Tomorrow night? Seven o'clock?"

"I'll be there."

And for the first time in a long time, Sander looked forward to a date.

Chapter Two

Lisa's hands shook as she packed up the last of her supplies, shepherded her nieces to the door, and left the rec center classroom. As Molly and Olivia chattered about making challah and how much fun the class had been, her mind wandered to one particular student.

Sander Fortune.

The man was gorgeous. Overgrown blond hair that begged her to run her hands through it and smooth it out. Or mess it up. Her cheeks heated. His hazel eyes twinkled when he grinned. She'd teased him just to see him smile. He towered over her, but instead of feeling intimidated, she felt safe. His large hands, useless at braiding challah, were tanned. And he smelled like rain.

She scoffed.

"What's wrong, Auntie Lisa?" Molly asked. "Didn't you think our challah looked the best?" As the older of the two girls, Molly was being particularly generous including her sister this time. Usually, that wasn't the case.

"Sorry, I was thinking about something else. Yes, you two made beautiful challah. I can't wait for your mom to see them." She opened her car door and helped them into their booster seats before circling around to the driver's side. All the while reminding herself to come back to reality. This wasn't the movies or a romance novel. This was *real life*. She didn't fall in lust at first sight, no matter how close to the surface her emotions were, or how delicious the man was. Except this time, she did. Her body had hummed each time she'd approached him. And her mind? Well, it had been fixated on him the entire class. It was a good thing everyone had paid for the event at registration, because she'd done a poor job of giving the other attendees the attention they deserved.

And she hadn't felt the usual peace she normally felt when she baked. For some, meditation helped center them. For her, it was baking. She'd get into a rhythm, her breathing would slow, and she'd end up with delicious food and a calm soul. Except today, the braided bread had done nothing for her psyche.

Even her nieces had noticed how her attention wavered. Luckily, at five and six years old, they were easily redirected, because she couldn't talk about her attraction with them. Their mother, on the other hand, was a different story. Stepping on the gas a little harder than usual, she drove as fast as was safely within the speed limit to her sister's house.

"Do you think Mommy will let us eat the challah when we get home, Auntie Lisa?" Olivia's voice interrupted Lisa's thoughts, and she glanced in the rearview mirror at the brown-haired cherub.

"I think she will once you bake it," she said. "Challah dough isn't like cake batter. It doesn't taste good raw."

The girls giggled and continued chattering to each other in the back seat, leaving Lisa free to let her mind wander yet again. Before she knew it, she had pulled into her sister's driveway and Sara came outside to greet them.

"Hey, there!" She leaned over and kissed the girls on their heads. "Did you have fun with Auntie Lisa?"

"Look what we made!" Molly held up her challah, and Olivia followed suit.

"Yummy!"

"Can we bake them now?" Olivia jumped up and down.

"Of course. Go put them in the kitchen, and I'll be right there."

As the girls rushed toward the house, Molly called back, "Auntie Lisa made a friend, Mommy!"

Lisa wanted to sink into the ground. Her face heated as Sara turned to her, eyebrows raised. This was not how she'd planned to start the conversation.

"You did?"

She fidgeted under her sister's stare. "Sander Fortune."

If Sara's eyebrows rose any farther, they'd blend into her hairline. "You're kidding. What was *he* doing at a challah-bake? He's not Jewish."

Shrugging, Lisa played with the cuffs of her shirtsleeves, pressing the edges like pie dough. "No idea. But, anyone can bake and eat challah, Sara. Being Jewish isn't a requirement." Even so, what *was* he doing there? He didn't seem to be much of a baker, as his lopsided challah demonstrated. The poor guy hadn't even known what challah *was* when he showed up. He'd said his daughter had signed him up. The question was…why?

"No, I know. It's just…a bit odd. He's gorgeous though."

Lisa glanced away. "He definitely won't crack any mirrors."

Her sister laughed. "As grandma would say, what a punim!"

"He asked me to dinner."

Sara grinned. "And you said…"

"I said yes. He's taking me to Captain's. Can you believe it? That place is crazy expensive."

"Then it's perfect for a first date."

Everyone in Emerald Ridge knew of Captain's. Located in the penthouse of the Emerald Ridge Hotel, it boasted panoramic views and ridiculously high prices. But the food was supposed to be excellent. Lisa couldn't afford it on a teacher's salary, but clearly, Sander Fortune didn't have that problem.

"Why do you say that?"

Sara shrugged. "Because a first date is to impress."

"Well, he's certainly got that covered. Oh God, what am I going to wear?"

Her sister wrapped her arm around her shoulders. "Come inside, I've got plenty of clothes you can look at."

"Hey, Lisa," David, Sara's husband, said as they crossed the living room and went upstairs.

"We're clothes shopping," Sara called over her shoulder.

"Oh boy." He laughed. "Have fun!"

Sara opened her large walk-in closet and flipped through the rack of hangers, muttering to herself. When she turned around, her arms were filled with outfits.

"Sara, I'm going on one date, not a ten-day cruise."

"You think this is all I'd pull if you were going on a cruise? Pfft. You need options. Get undressed."

As Lisa undressed, her nieces barged in. "Can we bake the challah now? Why is Auntie Lisa naked?" Olivia asked.

"Not yet, she's wearing underwear, and we're picking out an outfit for her."

"Oh, can we help?" Molly jumped up and down.

"I'd love your help, if you sit quietly over there," Lisa said.

Sara gave her a grateful smile. "Yes, go sit down, and you can be judges. We'll have a fashion show."

Lisa pulled a sparkly black bodysuit from the pile and paired it with wide-legged cream trousers.

"Mmm, no," Sara said, shaking her head. "Not quite right."

Lisa looked down at her legs. "Plus, if I spill on myself, it's totally going to show."

Next she tried on a one-shouldered dark green pantsuit.

"That's pretty," Olivia said.

Sara spun her hand in a circle. "Turn around."

Lisa did, taking a peek at her backside in the mirror. "Wearing this will make it hard to pee," she complained.

"And other things." Sara grinned.

"Not on a first date." Lisa injected pretend shock into her voice.

Sara laughed. "Now you sound like Mom."

"Oh jeez."

"Try on the sparkly blue one," Molly said. "I love sparkles."

Climbing out of the pantsuit, she pulled the dark blue wrap dress with silver threads woven through it over her head.

"That's it," Sara said before Lisa had a chance to finish zipping herself into it. "That's what you wear."

"*Now* can we make the challah?" Olivia asked.

Sara nodded. "Go downstairs and ask Daddy to preheat the oven. I'll be down in a sec." She turned to Lisa. "You look stunning."

Lisa stared at herself in the mirror. The wrap style accentuated her curves, and the V-neck showed off her cleavage.

"You don't think it's too revealing? Or too sparkly? I don't want to look cheap among all the wealthy diners."

The noise Sara made in response wasn't even close to ladylike. "You couldn't look cheap if you showed up in pink pleather and fake feathers. This is the dress that's going to make Sander Fortune drool."

Lisa nodded, turning from side to side and examining her reflection. The crepe fabric clung to her waist and flowed over her hips. She smoothed her hands down her sides. "You think so?"

"Trust me, if I could figure out a way to spy on you, I'd video it for you."

"God forbid."

Her sister laughed, then sobering, reached out and hugged her. "After everything you've gone through, sis, you deserve a little fun. So go out with Sander, have a wonderful dinner with him, and don't fret about anything beyond that."

Lisa swallowed. Fun? It had been a while since she'd let go and truly enjoyed herself. Maybe Sara was right. She glanced once again at her image in the mirror. This dress could definitely lead to fun. She threw her shoulders back, took a deep breath, and looked at her sister.

"Okay." No more worrying. It was time to live in the moment.

The next day, Sander called Kelsey as he stood in the kitchen, looking out at the patio while drinking his cup of coffee and munching on a slice of buttered challah.

"Hey, Kels. You have any free time today to come over and help me search for the boathouse key?" They'd discovered a secret door behind a sturdy partition wall last month while searching the boathouse, but it was only now that he had the time to look. Mark and Marlene had hidden a "family treasure" as a surprise for their kids, but had died in a car accident before anyone could find it. He'd bet a new ranch it was hidden behind the locked door. Why else would it be locked?

High-pitched voices in the background alerted him to the triplets' presence. He grinned. She'd taken to her new life like she was made for it.

"Yeah, how about during my lunch break."

"You get one of those?"

She laughed. "Very funny, Dad. I'll meet you at home around noon. I need to grab some more of my stuff too."

He loved how she still referred to this big house, now only occupied by him, as home. He squinted as he looked around the large kitchen and shuddered at the memory of walking in on her and Trevor fooling around. He hadn't meant to disturb them. Back when Kelsey still lived here with him in her wing of the main house, she'd brought guys she was seeing back home, but this was the first time he'd interrupted them making out.

"Guess I should be grateful it only happened that one time," he muttered as he washed out his coffee mug. Still, he wanted to scrub the image from his mind with bleach. She'd always be his little girl.

A few hours later, the front door opened.

"Dad?"

He met her in the foyer and kissed her cheek. "You want to get your things before or after we search?"

"After."

They stood in the foyer of the house, and Sander tried to survey the home from his brother's perspective. Back when Mark and Marlene built the home, they'd envisioned a summer home conclave that the family could enjoy forever. They'd built additional homes—more like McMansions—each time one of their children was born, never expecting they'd no longer be around to enjoy it. Or that he and Kelsey would move into their home after their deaths. If they were going to find the key, he had to put himself in his brother's shoes.

The wide and airy flagstone entry led directly into the living room, with a huge fireplace taking up one wall and, thanks to the open floor plan, into the kitchen and dining room. Sander thought the layout was perfect for a family, and it had enabled him and Delia, his housekeeper, to keep an eye on all the little ones from any one of those living spaces. He remembered when he'd first hired her, her eyes had rounded when she'd stepped into the foyer, and she'd murmured how large the house was. But when she saw the open floor plan, she'd nodded. Something had clicked, and she'd given him a smile of confidence. Now, however, trying to determine the best place to start seemed a little overwhelming. He really missed the woman, who'd become more of a friend than a housekeeper as the years went on.

"I think we should start in your office," Kelsey said, turning toward her right.

"My office? Why? I'm in there all the time and haven't found it yet."

She shrugged. "Because I think that's where anything of importance would be kept." She paused, a mischievous glint in her eye. "At least, that's what happens in all the movies."

He chuffed, and some of his anxiety about the second reason he'd asked her to come over disappeared. "Sure. Why not." He followed her into the study and scanned the room. Separated from the living room by an arched doorway, the white-walled room was fitted with floor-to-ceiling oak bookcases, a desk, and a drafting table, with cowhide chairs and a large leather sofa. Sander did most of his work here, and it also had a separate door to the outside, so clients and contractors could come to his office without having to walk through his home.

"Where do you want me to look?" she asked.

"How about you take that half of the room, and I'll take this half," he said, striding toward the desk.

"Got it, boss."

The physical distance between them helped calm the rest of his nerves. He silently berated himself as he opened drawers and looked for secret compartments. *Man up.* He cleared his throat.

"So, ah, do you know a woman named Lisa Bergen?" He held his breath, not understanding why he was so nervous broaching the subject. After all, his daughter had been signing him up for classes for weeks now in the hopes he'd meet someone.

"The name sounds familiar, but I don't think I know her. Why?"

"Because I met her at the challah—"

"Woo hoo, it *worked*!" Kelsey shrieked, jumping up from where she was peering under shelves and racing over to him. She grabbed him around the shoulders and gave him a fierce hug from behind. "I knew you'd meet someone, Dad. Wait…why do I know her name?"

"She taught the class."

"Ohhh, the teacher. I knew her name sounded familiar, but I didn't expect *that*," she said. "What's she like? Does she like you too?"

How to describe a gorgeous, sexy woman to his daughter, whose excitement was reminding him of the boisterous child she'd been, rather than the grown woman she'd become. His mind froze. There were only so many boundaries he was willing to cross. Somehow, he needed to translate Lisa's lustrous dark wavy hair, creamy skin, voluptuous curves, and liquid eyes into something suitable for his daughter. She might physically be an adult, but in his mind, she'd always be his little girl. It was safer to limit the details to Lisa's personality.

"She's warm and funny. Patient. Dotes on her nieces. Makes great challah." He nodded toward the kitchen. "I baked it last night. It's ugly, but tastes great." He cleared his throat. "And I guess she likes me, since she agreed to go out with me tonight."

Kelsey's green eyes widened. "You asked her out on a date? All by yourself?"

Sander growled. His daughter, as usual, was stretching his frustration levels to their limits. "What do you mean, *by myself*? I'm a forty-four-year-old man and have been dating since before you were born. I am perfectly capable of asking a beautiful woman out to dinner."

Kelsey flashed a wicked grin. "You're also so easy to play."

He groaned. "You're grounded."

"Okay, Dad. Where are you taking her?"

"Captain's."

"Ooh, fancy. You're really turning on the charm."

He moved from the desk to the built-in filing cabinets beneath the bookcases. What were the chances someone had hidden a key in the *K* section? And more importantly, what made him start this conversation with his daughter? You'd think he'd learn by now. She was always teasing him, and heck, she'd learned it from him. But this time, being on the receiving end of her quips made him fidget.

Her shadow crossed his line of sight, startling him. "I'm just teasing you," she said. "I think it's great you asked her to dinner, and anyone would be impressed by Captain's. Worst case, you both get a nice meal."

He smiled at her, ruefully. "It's better than having to cook."

She laughed. "True. If she's the woman I'm picturing, I think I've seen her around town a couple times. With a man at one point, but that was a long time ago. She might be divorced, or widowed? I haven't seen her with anyone in…gosh, it's been years." She looked at her dad. "She's probably as happy to get out of cooking as you are."

Shrugging, Sander shut the file cabinet door. "I don't know, but she makes damn fine challah." The yeasty aroma had filled his home last night and lingered into this morning, making him sigh in pleasure. And despite how lopsided it looked, it tasted amazing.

She rolled her eyes. "Do you know what she does for a living?"

"Other than teach the challah-baking class? I don't. I guess I'll have to ask tonight." He didn't know a whole lot about her. Just how she made him feel. As he searched his side of the study, bits and pieces from yesterday's class filtered through his mind. She'd glowed when she put her arms around her nieces, and pride made her eyes shine when she'd examined their challah.

Sam chuffed. Theirs had looked significantly better than his.

He'd been kind of awed by her ability to teach the adults while still paying attention to her young nieces. Sander remembered his daughter at that age, gap-toothed smile and all. He'd raised her on his own since she was a month old, and they'd had a "two of them against the world" attitude for the first three years of her life, until his nieces and nephews, along with his housekeeper's son, had joined his household. And he couldn't be sure, but at least in his opinion, kids took up a *lot* of attention. Lisa clearly was talented.

Sitting back on his haunches, he braced his hands on his thighs and pushed himself up to standing. "Kels, you having any luck?"

"Nope. By the way, I'm noticing a distinct lack of Christmas decorations."

He shrugged. "I'm not much in the mood this year."

"Unacceptable." She shook her head. "I'm rounding up the family and we're coming over to decorate. You're the one who insists on all of us getting together for family dinners at least once a month. Well, this time, we're decorating while we eat."

"It's not necessary. I didn't get a tree—"

"We'll pick one out," she interrupted.

"And dragging all those boxes from the attic..." Just the thought of it tired him out.

"We'll take care of everything, I promise. All you have to do is provide the space." She spread her arms wide. "Which you have. Leave the rest to me. Besides, Linc would want us to..."

He glared at her use of the "Linc card," something she knew would make him cave. Linc always got joy out of Christmas celebrations. As a child, Linc had been the first one to sit by the Christmas tree on Christmas morning, his bouncing leg the only indication of how eager he was for everyone else to arrive to open presents. Sander gave in. Turning in place, he scanned the room. "I don't think we're going to find anything in here. Not sure where to look next, but I need a break."

She rose and met him in the center of the room. The red, blue and gray Oriental rug muffled her footsteps. "And you need time to get ready for your date, while I go get more of my stuff to take over to Trevor's."

He laughed at the googly eyes she made at him. "Oh brother."

"Don't tell me you're not going to dress nicely for Lisa."

"What do you take me for? An idiot? Of course I'm going to dress nicely. This isn't my first rodeo, you know."

He'd dated plenty of women in the past few years, now that all the kids were grown, and he'd dressed appropriately for all of them, especially the first dates. The fact that none of them had developed into relationships had less to do with what he wore and more to do with cross-purposes, he suspected. Either the women he dated didn't like the idea of being a stepmother to five children—even if those five children were old enough to take care of themselves—or they wanted babies of their own.

No thank you. Been there, done that. He loved his large family. Hell, he'd die for them if necessary. But he wasn't about to start over again. Spending time with his kids and their families was rewarding and fun and gave him the chance to enjoy all the chaos and then retreat to his own quiet home when he'd had enough. He loved seeing his daughter, nieces, and nephews grow and develop fulfilling relationships.

As for him? Who knew? But a thrill of excitement raced down his spine at the prospect of his date with Lisa. And for the moment, that was enough.

"Mrs. Bergen, my mom just had a baby!"

Lisa whipped her head up from where she'd been focusing on her computer and stared at her fourth-period student, who'd lingered after the bell rang. The sixth-grade girl's eyes shone with excitement, and a slash of jealousy stabbed at Lisa. She blinked, pushing it out of reach, and smiled.

"Morgan, that's wonderful! Congratulations! Boy or girl?"

Morgan walked over, holding out a photo. "Boy. His name is Aiden. Isn't he cute?"

The image of the squished red face, tiny blue cap, and swaddled body made Lisa's heart ache with longing.

"He's..." She cleared her throat and tried again.

"He's beautiful." She handed back the photo and glanced at the clock over her classroom door. "Is your mom home from the hospital yet?"

Morgan shook her head. "Tomorrow. My grandparents are staying with us until then."

Her bubbly pupil had an older brother and younger sister. It was going to be a full house. "How nice to have a baby with you for Christmas," Lisa said. "Do you or your family need anything?"

"We're good. My mom's friends started a meal train for us, plus my grandparents will stay for a week after my mom comes home. I can't wait," she said, staring at the photo of her brother. "Although I kinda wish he was a girl."

Lisa suppressed a laugh. "He's still adorable, and you're a very lucky big sister. Please send my congratulations to your family. Now, you'd better get to your next class before you're marked late."

Putting the photo in her backpack, Morgan slung the bag over her shoulder, waved goodbye, and left the classroom.

Lisa took deep breaths and thanked the scheduling gods that she had a free fifth period. She walked to the window and looked out over the schoolyard, not really seeing anything except the image of Morgan's new brother. She wrapped her arms around her stomach. Would she ever get her chance to be a mom?

This was the hardest part about being a teacher, at least for her. With so many students, there was always someone whose mom was pregnant. Just last week, during parent-teacher conferences, she'd had three mothers tell her their good news.

Straightening her shoulders, she vowed she wasn't going to wallow in this anymore. She had too much to do before her date tonight. And after that date? Well, she was looking at her options.

That night, she pulled on her sister's sparkly blue dress, hands shaking. What was she doing, going out with Sander Fortune, of all people? She'd never dated anyone who didn't have some connection to someone she knew. Meeting a random stranger wasn't her thing, so she'd relied on setups and "friend of a friend" dates. That's how she'd met Jordan, and that's what she'd done for the few dates she'd been on since his death. It was safe and comfortable and gave her a good start to the conversation, since they could talk about their mutual acquaintance, as well as any common interests they'd been told they had.

But one look at Sander with his hands covered in sticky challah dough, and she'd forgotten all her dating rules. Heck, she was lucky she remembered the challah recipe. He'd pinned her with his twinkly-eyed gaze, and she was ready to say yes to anything he suggested. Her cheeks burned. Thank goodness, all he'd asked her for was a dinner date.

A dinner date at one of, if not the, nicest places in town. Then again, he was a Fortune, what did she expect? McDonald's? She sank onto her bed. Oh god, he was a Fortune. So out of her league. It didn't matter what her sister said about living in the moment. Her sister wasn't the one stepping so far out of her comfort zone she was practically entering into orbit. Sweat popped on her skin, and she fanned herself. All she needed was to stain this dress and then she'd have nothing to wear.

What had gotten into her?

And why did her insides flutter every time she thought about Sander? She had never been a "fall in lust" kind of woman. *Ever.* Attraction, like love, developed over time. She was more concerned with their minds and their personalities than their looks. But with Sander? Heat had flooded her the first time he'd turned his hazel-eyed stare to her. She hadn't been able to stop looking at his large, masculine hands as they kneaded the dough. Ugh! She couldn't do this. She *shouldn't* do this.

She had to cancel. She'd plead some sort of emergency that was vague enough not to tempt fate, but specific enough not to offend him. She nodded. Yeah, cancel.

Her phone rang, and relief washed over her. Maybe he was canceling first.

She reached for it, but her relief disappeared when she saw her mom's caller ID on the screen.

"Hi, Mom."

"You don't sound happy to hear from me, Lis. Were you hoping for someone else?"

"Not exactly."

Her mom laughed. "Well, I wanted to wish you luck on your date. Sara told me."

A knot formed in the pit of her stomach. "Thanks. I'm not sure it's a good idea though."

"Why not?"

"Because I know nothing about him. I've basically

accepted a date from a random stranger off the street."
A super wealthy, gorgeous stranger.

Her mom gave an understanding huff. "Sander Fortune, right?"

"Yeah. He took my challah-baking class."

"I knew his brother, Mark, and sister-in-law, Marlene. They were lovely people. We knew each other from their summer visits here." Her mom paused a moment. "Such a shame. They were killed in an accident, orphaning their four children. Sander took them in and raised them along with his young daughter."

Lisa's heart pattered against her ribs even as her eyes filled with tears. "Five children? That's...amazing." Sympathy overwhelmed her. What a loss they'd all experienced. They *did* have something in common. And at the same time, her mind exploded with possibilities. He was a *family* man. Without warning, all the fantasies she'd had about raising children rushed to the forefront of her mind. She tried to push the excitement down.

"That poor man."

"He's done a good job with them. Even helped to raise his housekeeper's son, Linc Banning."

"Wait, why does that name sound familiar?" Lisa asked.

Her mother tsked. "He was found shot to death by the river back in July."

Lisa inhaled. "That's right. Oh my gosh, how horrible." No matter how well-off that family was, it hadn't protected them from loss. She didn't recall seeing any obvious signs of mourning when she'd met Sander, but she knew better than anyone that some pain never went away. Her chest tightened. "I wonder if they caught the person who did it?"

"I haven't heard anything," her mom said.

Lisa began putting on jewelry, pausing in the middle of fastening one earring. "I've never felt such instant attraction to anyone." She lowered her voice. "Not even to Jordan, and I adored him. I feel guilty being attracted to Sander."

"Oh, honey, Jordan wouldn't want you to feel guilty. Every relationship is different. You know he'd want you to move on."

"I know he would, but it's hard. I've barely dated since he died, and the few dates I went on made me realize I'm more interested in having kids than a husband. Maybe I shouldn't go. I don't want to be unfair to Sander either."

"Lisa Bergen, you absolutely *must* go. Don't chicken out now without at least giving the man a chance. I did not raise a quitter, nor did I raise someone with the manners of a schlub."

Her mom's stern words had the desired effect, and Lisa straightened her spine.

"You're right," she said, sighing softly. "I can't back out now." She stared at her reflection in the mirror, wondering what Sander would think.

She'd tamed her long, dark hair with lots more hair product than she usually used, resulting in it looking less like a wild rat's nest than it did during the miserable heat of a Texas summer and more like a full, wavy cascade. She peered closely at it. She'd found a gray hair the other day and plucked it out before it had a chance to sprout any friends.

Thanks to tips from her sister, she'd created the perfect smoky eye and used a hint of gloss on her naturally pink lips. Diamond stud earrings and a silver necklace, as well as silver slingbacks took her out of her daily "teacher look" and into her "night out on the town guise." She exhaled, knowing she looked the part.

Now she just had to *act* it.

"Worst case, I get a good meal out of this."

"Best case, you have a good time with another adult," her mom added.

Lisa laughed. "What exactly do you mean by 'good time,' Mom?"

"Nope, not falling for that one. Not discussing what you do or don't do with an attractive man. La-la-la-la-la! I can't hear you."

"You do know your other daughter has children. And you know how you make them."

"Lisa, I'm warning you..."

She laughed. "I'm just giving you a hard time. I love you."

"Love you, too, even if you provide me way too many details. Now go have fun."

Hanging up the phone, Lisa grabbed her purse and headed to the restaurant, excitement quickening her steps. Because, despite all her reservations, she couldn't avoid the flashes of hope that sparked to life the more she thought of Sander. He was a family man, he was drop-dead gorgeous, and he was single. Maybe her dreams of having a child—or several—weren't as unattainable as she thought.

Chapter Three

When Lisa arrived at Captain's, she handed her keys to the valet and entered the ornate lobby of the Emerald Ridge Hotel. Huge red and silver foil-wrapped presents framed the entryway. Giant fir boughs surrounded the marble fireplace on one side of the space, and wreaths with red balls and candy canes decorated every carved doorway. And to her surprise—and delight—a fancy silver electric menorah sat on the mahogany reservation desk. Sleek but comfortable cream velvet sofas were clustered around marble and mahogany tables.

Even the hotel guests looked fancy—the men in expensive suits, the women with sparkly jewelry and lavish shoes. Tourism was brisk in Emerald Ridge, and all the well-to-do tourists stayed at the Emerald Ridge Hotel. The only times she'd been here were for a bridal shower or two. She tried to keep her mouth from falling open as she took one last glance around the lobby before she headed to the elevator.

Riding it to the top floor, she stepped out into the private restaurant's marble foyer. Once again, Christmas decorations added festivity to the well-appointed area, but up here, twinkle lights illuminated every door and window frame, and holiday melodies played through invisible speakers. Peeking inside the restaurant, she admired the dark wood paneling on two sides of the restaurant, floor-to-ceiling windows on the third side, and mirrored shelves with top-shelf bottles of alcohol along the fourth wall. Wall sconces and fancy track lighting added even more ambience to the seafood restaurant. She couldn't wait to enter and explore the menu.

She stood at the large windows overlooking downtown Emerald Ridge while fighting the swarm of butterflies taking flight in her stomach. She was about to go on a date with Sander Fortune! Trying to relax, she admired the view. During the day, with the bright sun reflecting off the white limestone buildings covered with bougainvillea, it was a lovely sight. Now, with the moon shining, lending everything a silvery glow, it was hauntingly beautiful. Tiny multicolored Christmas lights turned the limestone a rainbow of colors.

Lisa was just about to look for Sander inside the restaurant when a deep voice resonated close to her ear.

"Good evening."

She turned. Her eyes widened at his black Stetson, crisp white shirt beneath a black leather jacket, a bolo tie with a green moss agate, and black jeans with silver cowboy boots. The agate's color made his hazel eyes glow. His square jaw was clean-shaven, his blond hair tucked behind his ear. He looked *delicious*. She swallowed.

"Hello." Her voice sounded breathless, like she'd just run a marathon.

His gaze left a trail of heat as he took in all of her, and his face softened in approval. It had been a long time since she'd elicited that kind of appreciation in a man, and she silently thanked her sister for the dress.

"I hope you weren't waiting long," he said.

"No. I just got here. I was admiring the view."

"Me too," he murmured, his gaze locked on her.

Her cheeks flushed.

He held out a hand to her, his fingers tightening around hers as he led her toward the restaurant. His grip was firm, his stride sure, and she felt tiny walking next to him. That never happened, not with her curves. She kind of liked it.

Inside the restaurant, the maître d' led them across plush carpeting that muffled their footsteps to their white-linen-covered table by the floor-to-ceiling window, and waited while Sander held her chair before sitting across from her. Her anticipation increased as a waiter materialized at their side and poured their water, while another handed them large, leather-bound menus. Finally, when all was prepared, they left Lisa and Sander to themselves.

"I hope you don't mind that I met you here," he said, "rather than picked you up. My daughter tells me it's preferable to give the woman an escape route on the first date."

Lisa laughed. "Your daughter is correct." She paused. "Although I'm hoping I won't need one."

"I'll try to be on my best behavior."

He winked, making a frisson of desire skate through her. She loved a man with a deprecating sense of humor.

"Are you ever on *bad* behavior?"

He leaned forward, resting his muscular forearms on the table. "Guess that depends on who you ask. My family would probably regale you with lots of tales sure to make you question why you agreed to tonight."

She nodded. "I've never been to Captain's before." She looked around the dining room, but her gaze darted back to Sander at his burst of laughter.

Her mouth dropped. "Oh my goodness, I did *not* mean to imply that was the reason for my saying yes. Talk about a horrible segue."

When he calmed, he reached across the table and squeezed her hand. "So, tell me why you *did* agree."

There were a million reasons she could give, all of which would keep a safe distance between them, but instead, she went with the truth. Whether they were going to start a romantic relationship or a friendship or just an acquaintanceship, it had to be built on honesty. "You were funny, and not a lot of people have made me laugh recently."

His eyes darkened with understanding. "I like a woman with a good sense of humor. Humor's gotten me through a lot of trying times over the years as well."

"My mother mentioned you were a single dad. I'll bet laughter helped with that."

He grinned. "A lot. I've been raising kids since I was twenty-one. In fact, now that my daughter has moved into her own home with her fiancé and his triplets, and my nephew Harris is out of my house and divides his time between Dallas and his new wife's place in town, I'm finally an empty nester."

Part of Lisa's brain registered the multiple houses and the differences between her lifestyle and his. But the majority of her brain homed in on the triplets. As usual, whenever babies were mentioned, Lisa's chest tightened with longing. Before she could ask about the triplets, the waiter returned. "Would either of you like drinks or an appetizer?"

She brought her hand to her chest. "I'm so sorry, I haven't even looked at the menu yet." Great, did such an upscale restaurant expect people to stick to a timeline? She took a deep breath. It didn't matter. Impressing the waitstaff wasn't what she was here to do.

Sander turned to the waiter. "I'll take a scotch. Lisa, would you like a drink?"

Her worries dissolved as her handsome dinner date put her immediately at ease. "A glass of Cabernet if you have it," she said.

She studied Sander as he consulted the wine menu and discussed options with the waiter. She rarely perused wine menus, opting for whatever the waiter brought her. But Sander was clearly a wine connoisseur.

Then again, maybe he was asking about the scotch. She really should pay more attention.

After another moment, the waiter left with their drink order.

"We should probably figure out what we want to eat," she said. "I don't want to inconvenience him."

A soft look crossed Sander's face. She didn't know why, but it made him more approachable. More man, less *Fortune*. The butterflies in her stomach disappeared.

"Good idea."

His deep voice did something to her. She wasn't exactly sure what, but she wanted him to keep talking.

She opened the leather monstrosity and tried not to gape at the meals and their prices. Grilled wild king salmon for sixty-five dollars? So this was what it was like to be a Fortune…or to *have* one.

He looked over the top of his menu. "I've eaten the lobster and the sea bass before, and both are excellent."

Both of them were also expensive, but her heart melted a little when she realized he might be telling her not to worry about prices. This was a date, and she was going to relax. Finally deciding on the Chilean sea bass with rice and asparagus, she closed her menu and rested it off to the side.

"Would you like to split an appetizer or two?" Sander leaned forward. "Their gougères with smoked salmon, caviar and prosciutto is fantastic."

She glanced at the menu again, having no idea what the appetizer was, but knowing she liked salmon and caviar. She was a foodie after all, and therefore, up for the challenge.

"Okay."

His hazel eyes had flecks of gold in them, and they sparkled when he smiled. Small lines at the outer edges of his eyes sprouted as well, and she swallowed. She was a sucker for eye lines…at least as long as they were on someone else's face. Preferably a man's. Pity how women looked old and men looked distinguished... and sexy as hell.

Once the waiter returned with their drinks and took their order, Lisa asked the question that had dominated her thoughts since the interruption.

"You started raising kids at twenty-one? That must have been rough, being such a young father."

He smiled, satisfaction making his shoulders straighten. "It was tough, and nothing I ever expected, but probably one of the most rewarding things I've ever done."

Joy crept into her chest. Her instincts were right—he *was* a family man. And a happy one at that.

"May I ask what happened?"

He leaned forward, folding his forearms on the table. The action made his powerful shoulders fill out the sleeves of his shirt, and she sighed.

"I dated Kelsey's mother while I was in college." His expression grew wistful. "She was lovely. Kelsey reminds me of her, especially her auburn hair and green eyes." He paused, a faraway expression on his face.

Lisa waited. She had her own memories of first meeting Jordan, and no matter how sad it was that their life together had ended, those memories still brought her joy.

Sander cleared his throat and continued. "I guess we weren't as careful as we should have been, and Lani got pregnant. When she told me, I wasn't sure I was ready to be a dad, but I knew my responsibility and stepped up. Once I went with her to the first doctor's appointment, I was all in. Seeing the baby on the sonogram..."

Lisa's felt a pang in her chest. She remembered that moment as if it were yesterday. The joy and awe slicing through her, the sudden realization that this was real. She'd never seen such a look of awe on Jordan's face before, not even when he caught his first glimpse of her on their wedding day.

Shaking his head, Sander admitted gruffly, "Looking back now, I was always more into the pregnancy than Lani was, but I attributed her reaction to the hormones." He shrugged. "I should have known or had some inkling things were off."

Lisa's mouth dropped, and even though she barely knew the man, she couldn't stay silent. "How *could* you have known?"

"She was always a free spirit. And even after Kelsey was born, she strained against the bonds that forced her to lose her freedom. Ultimately, she couldn't handle the idea of settling down, and left." He looked away for a minute, and her heart ached for the two of them.

"I'll admit, a part of me was relieved that I could continue on my own, doing what I thought was best for my daughter, but there was also a part of me that wished she'd stayed. Kelsey deserved to have a mother who cared enough to stick around." He sighed, and once again, sympathy for his plight overwhelmed her.

"You're right, she did." Lisa couldn't understand how anyone could just up and abandon their family. "But at least she had you, and I'm sure you were an amazing father."

He cleared his throat and gave her a grateful smile. "Anyway, about a month after she was born, her mother died in a car accident, and I officially became a single dad."

Lisa's mouth dropped. "Oh my god. That's just awful—for all of you." She took a sip of her water to recover from the thought. "But as I said, Kelsey's lucky to have you."

Sander nodded. "Thank you. But the way I see it, we were lucky to have each other."

"You both went through an awful lot. I'm not sure most twentysomethings would be able to step up like you did."

Sander leaned forward, his gaze fierce. "I did what I had to do. I would never have chosen how things happened, but I don't regret a single thing."

"Your family must be very proud of you."

"I don't know about proud, but they stepped up and helped me as much as they could. Kelsey and I managed pretty well. And thanks to them, I made it through school. But then my brother and sister-in-law were killed in a car accident, orphaning their four kids, and I got custody."

The responsibility might have destroyed someone weaker, but Sander's strength and honor oozed from every pore. As much as she'd been attracted to him before, she admired him even more.

"Oh my gosh. I can't believe you did that on your own."

"What was I supposed to do? Ignore them?" He fiddled with the rim of his water glass. "I couldn't do that. I took them in, hired a housekeeper, who also had a young son." He gave a sheepish grin. "We all became one big happy family."

"Talk about a full house," Lisa said. She envied the bustle as much as her heart ached for the tragedy they all suffered. "I have a sister, and growing up, we were quite a handful. I can only imagine the chaos you experienced."

He gave a quick laugh. "You have no idea."

"Where is everyone now?" She grew wistful. "You must have amazing family get-togethers."

"When my brother and sister-in-law bought the property where I live now, they built houses for each of their children as they were born. So they all have homes close by, although not everyone lives there full-time." He sobered. "And Linc, my housekeeper's son, was killed a few months back." He shook his head. "I wish I knew what happened."

Just when she was starting to think of Sander without the "Fortune" attached to his name, he mentioned a family compound, and her stomach churned with anxiety once again. But then he reminded her about the housekeeper's son, and her heartbeat slowed.

This poor man.

"I heard about that," Lisa said, voice soft, eyes welling again. "I'm so sorry."

He cleared his throat. "Enough about me. Tell me about yourself."

She took a deep breath. "I'm widowed." She swallowed, but continued. "I teach at the middle school. And I love to cook."

He smiled. "Clearly. And you're a good one too."

"Thank you."

"I'm sorry about your husband. I know how hard it is to lose someone."

Sympathy shone from his eyes, wrapped around her shoulders, and comforted her. He really *did* understand.

"It is, and thanks to my friends and family, I'm finally starting to get out from under that cloud."

"It's hard," he said thickly. "And it takes a while. But middle school? Wow. I don't envy you. All those hormones would drive me crazy. *Did* drive me crazy!"

She laughed. "I love kids, but I'll admit, those raging hormones can be a challenge."

"What subject do you teach?"

"English. We're currently in our Shakespeare unit."

He drew back in horror, but the twinkle in his eye let her know he was teasing. "Oh gosh, I hated reading Shakespeare."

She rose, pretending to leave, then laughed at his shocked expression and sat back down. "You'd love it if I were teaching it."

Sander met her gaze and heat flared in his eyes, darkening them to a molten gold. Lisa struggled to breathe.

"I bet I would," he said. The pitch of his voice, low and deep, sent tremors down her spine.

The waiter arrived with their appetizer, dousing the heat rising between them. Disappointment mixed with relief, and Lisa used the break to compose herself while placing the napkin on her lap. She turned her focus to the item Sander had ordered. He served her and then himself, and she silently gave him points for manners.

Not that he needed them.

The cheesy puffs looked delicious and tasted even better. She moaned, and his stare bored into her.

"This is heaven," she murmured

"You're right."

She looked at him askance, even though the English teacher in her appreciated his double entendre. "You haven't tried it yet."

A glimmer of a smile crossed his face as his gaze remained locked on her. After another moment passed, he blinked and tasted the appetizer. The muscles of his jaw clenched as he chewed, and she tightened her grip on the fork. He licked his lips, and her breath hitched. Then he swallowed, as did she.

"Delicious," he said.

She reached for her glass of wine and took a large sip, trying to force her attention elsewhere. His eyes gleamed as if he could read her thoughts. That was a scary prospect. Although so far, everything had been so easy between them. She hadn't once felt that moment of anxiety, of "what do I say now?"

"How about you?" she asked. "Do you enjoy your work?"

"I do," he said. "I'm an architect, specializing in designing or remodeling ranches."

Lisa's laugh interrupted him, and she apologized. "It's just, that's so right for a Fortune."

He nodded. "I hear you. We're all involved in ranch life in some way, some of us more directly than others. But I was always fascinated with the building and planning and design of things. I grew up with a sketchbook practically attached to my body."

"So you're not into cattle and horses."

He chuckled. "Well, they're in my blood, so yes, just a little differently than some others in my family are."

Her chest tightened. "That must have been really hard."

"It was. Thank God they've all turned out okay. Except..." His eyes darkened and pain twisted his features.

"Linc?"

He gave her a look filled with relief. "I'm sorry. That's not exactly good first-date conversation."

She shrugged. "I think we both understand loss, and it's only natural to talk about things that affect you."

His ability to feel the same emotions she did, to understand on a visceral level, what she experienced, drew her to him even more deeply. And although she didn't want him to hurt, she appreciated and admired his ability to show it. When Jordan died, she'd walled herself off from everyone. While the immediacy of her grief had passed, it felt good to be able to step back into the light.

"May I ask what happened to your husband?" Sander's voice was gentle. Normally, she didn't like discussing Jordan with strangers. But Sander's baring of his pain had made him less of a stranger, more of a friend, and this time, she wanted to open up about it.

"He had a heart attack. Out of the blue. One of those 'widow-makers.'" The shock and grief had slashed through her soul. Even now, thinking about that day gutted her. But knowing Sander had experienced the loss of loved ones too lessened the pain somehow.

"That must have been horrible," he said. "I remember the jagged pain when my brother and sister-in-law were killed suddenly. It's like plunging off a cliff into an abyss."

The waiter appeared once again with their meals, and they stopped speaking until he left.

She'd likened it to having a bucket of icy cold water poured over your head, but Sander's description worked just as well. "It was…" She swirled her finger over the linen tablecloth. "I miscarried a month later. I don't know if it just wasn't meant to be, or if it was from the shock of losing Jordan, but I think I went a little crazy afterward."

Pain shadowed Sander's face, mirroring her own thoughts. "When Lani disappeared then was killed in that car accident after giving birth, I remember the agony of knowing my child would never experience a mother's love. I know it's not the same—"

Lisa interrupted. "No, but I think the pain is similar. You have that hope that blossomed just snuffed out."

"And in its place is this…void. You don't want to examine it too closely, but it's filled with pain and regret and abandonment."

Her eyes filled, and she blinked the tears away. He got her. He got everything about her. This man…

He reached across the table and squeezed her hand. His grasp offered safety and compassion. Heat zipped along her arm and wrapped her body in warmth. In his kind eyes, his solid presence, the life she'd always wanted burst into her mind—a husband to share the burden, children to bring joy. But more than just a vision, it burst into life, like the moment in *The Wizard of Oz* when the film switched from black and white to Technicolor. Children's laughter echoed in her head. The scent of baby powder and home-cooked meals wafted around her. A vision of the two of them walking arm in arm after putting their kids to bed played before her mind's eye.

"I never pictured myself alone, and after Jordan died, I… I was. So desperately alone. I hated that." She fisted her hand on the table. "I've always been independent, but that loneliness, it went bone-deep."

He nodded, like he understood, and she realized he did. "And the few times I ventured out, tried to reenter the world, it was as if everyone but me had a purpose, a person, a family. At first, I just assumed it was grief, that even though it *seemed* as if my dreams of a family were shattered, the possibility still existed."

She shrugged. "But even though the immediate grief lessened, that hopelessness didn't. I've dated some, but nothing really gelled, and I realized that I haven't been able to get rid of this baby fever. I might be alone, or I might meet someone, but regardless, I need children in my life. And lately, now that I'm thirty-eight, I've been looking into other options, like IVF and maybe even adoption."

The words tumbled out before she could stop them. Embarrassment heated her cheeks, but it quickly gave way to a sense of peace. She and Sander had clicked from the moment they first saw each other in her challah-baking class. They were perfect for each other, as their dinner conversation had proved. If she couldn't tell him, who *could* she tell?

Except…his hand spasmed in hers. After a long moment, he released his grip.

"IVF is expensive," she conceded. "I can't see how I can afford it on my teacher's salary. But, my sister suggested adoption, and I'm kind of leaning toward it. There are so many children who need a good home. What do you think?"

"I've heard IVF can bankrupt people," he said, his voice cooler than it had been before. Did he think she'd agreed to this date because of his money? She inhaled, annoyance flaring inside. But just as quickly as it appeared, it faded. Sander Fortune probably had a lot of experience with people who were after his money, and he didn't know her well.

How hard must it be to wonder if every person who befriends you is interested in you for yourself or for your bank account?

Sympathy replaced her annoyance.

She nodded. "I totally understand how that can happen. There's no way I can afford it, especially since it's not even guaranteed on the first try. And to have to deal with not only the disappointment of a failed attempt along with the economic stress of the procedure, well, that's not for me. But adoption…"

Sander remained silent, his gaze focused on the fish on his plate. As his shoulders rose, Lisa's appetite waned. Maybe she hadn't been clear enough? But how exactly does one say, "Don't worry, I'm not here because you're rich." *I mean, I guess I could say that, but, really?*

The longer he remained silent, though, the more her mental chatter echoed. Maybe he wasn't thinking about whether or not she was a gold digger. Had she scared him off? Talking about babies on a first date probably wasn't the wisest choice of topics. But he'd been so easy to talk to. Even so...maybe she should have kept her mouth shut about her desire for a baby.

Now she wanted to sink beneath the table and hide.

He exhaled, his muscular chest straining the buttons of his shirt. "I think there are a lot of kids out there in need of good homes."

That didn't tell her anything. "It sounds like there's a *but* in there somewhere."

His shoulders lowered. "I've got to be honest with you, Lisa. I don't want any more kids. Ever."

Her stomach dropped. *What?*

"I've spent the last twenty-three years raising five kids. My daughter just moved out last month, and even still, she's back and forth between her new home and mine. I'm finally done with all that, finally able to be free. I don't want to give that up."

His voice was gentle but firm, and somewhere behind the words, Lisa knew she wouldn't be able to change his mind.

Disappointment filled her mouth with bitterness, like the horseradish during the Passover seder. She swallowed, trying not to let on how much his answer bothered her.

"I see," she said. She stared at her plate, unable to eat

another morsel of the fish, no matter how tasty it had been only moments before. This was another reason she wished they'd gone someplace more in her budget. She didn't need the guilt she'd feel, letting this expensive meal go to waste.

"I'm sorry," he said, his husky tone grating over every nerve in her body.

She gave him a sad smile. "Don't be. You've raised your share of children, and you deserve some well-earned freedom."

The silence stretched between them, odd because they hadn't stopped talking since they arrived.

Thank goodness, the waiter reappeared. Was he tuned into their awkwardness or did he have a timer set for frequency of checking on dinner guests? Lisa would have laughed, but she was afraid any emotion she showed would end up with her bursting into tears.

"Would you like that wrapped to go?" he asked her.

She nodded.

"Can I interest either of you in dessert? We have a chocolate lava cake that is to die for, if I do say so myself."

Sander leaned toward her, but before he had a chance to speak, she shook her head. "No, thank you. I'm full."

He looked as if he wanted to argue with her, but instead, turned to the waiter and requested the check.

She had no idea what they talked about for the next five minutes as they wrapped up their date. Lisa assumed she spoke and gave correct answers, but her heart wasn't in it, and her mind was fixated on how fast this evening had gone from perfection to…nothing.

Once again, her hopes of finding a man who shared her dreams were dashed.

Outside the hotel, the cool evening air brought her out of her thoughts and back to reality.

"Thank you for a lovely dinner," she said, giving him what she hoped was a smile.

"Thank you for joining me." His eyes had lost that glimmer, and those sexy lines in the corners were gone. He looked almost disappointed.

"I should get home," she said, searching her purse for her valet ticket.

"Me too." He leaned toward her and placed a gentle kiss on her cheek. She closed her eyes, inhaling his spicy scent, wishing with all her heart it could be different.

"Will you text me when you get back, just so I know you're safe?" he asked.

She nodded.

As her car pulled up, she climbed inside and gave him a wave before driving off. As he and the crazy expensive hotel with the restaurant she'd probably never eat in again faded into the distance, she gave herself a stern shake. She hadn't gone into this date with any expectations. Well, not *too* many. As wonderful as Sander had been, he was no different than the other men she'd dated since Jordan died. No matter how let down she might feel, her time would be better spent focusing on how to become a mom, rather than on the sexy man she almost fell for.

Even if her cheek still burned from his lips.

Chapter Four

After a restless evening that he'd spent tossing and turning, Sander sat at his desk in his home office the next morning, working on initial drawings for a client who wanted to buy and completely redesign an existing ranch about a hundred miles away. The cool winter sun slanted through the window, casting a cold light across the Oriental carpet and onto the wide-plank wood floors. He tapped the edge of his tablet in frustration as he stared through the arched doorway into the living room, dissatisfied with the changes he proposed for the layout.

There was nothing wrong with his suggestions per se. Each one would update the hundred-year-old ranch and bring it into the modern era just fine. And that was the problem. The drawing was fine. It just wasn't unique or awe-inspiring or even good.

Gripping the ends of his hair and pulling, he opened up a new file on his tablet, prepared to start over in the hopes of infusing his proposal with the wow factor. But instead of focusing on the task at hand, thoughts of last night's date distracted him. Both times he and Lisa had been together, sparks flew. Their chemistry was undeniable. His body responded to her in ways he hadn't experienced in years. Her vanilla scent, her throaty laugh, the smooth feel of her skin, her luscious curves in her petite frame... He groaned and tried to get his brain to engage and return to work.

But it was useless.

Because she'd responded to him in much the same way. Knowing she was attracted to him as much as he was to her made reality all the more difficult. He'd enjoyed himself last night, so much so that over their appetizer, he'd even entertained thoughts of follow-up dates so they could spend more time together. That had never happened to him before. He'd dated on and off over the years, but never anyone whom he jibed with. But Lisa? Her humor, her intelligence... He shook his head. She was complex. Even their shared sorrows had bonded them together.

Once again he turned back to his tablet and almost threw it across the room. Fate was against him, it seemed, because this client wanted nursery space and baby animal breeding areas. Which led him back to thoughts of Lisa.

Her strong desire for children had surprised him. Why, he didn't know. She was still young enough to have them on her own, and she was fantastic with them. He'd witnessed her patience with her nieces at the rec center when they'd made challah. So her desire to have children wasn't what shocked him. It was the way she'd *described* that desire, the fire in her eyes, the stridency in her voice that had taken him aback. He certainly didn't begrudge her wanting a family, but he didn't want to be a part of it.

Disappointment shot through him, surprising him with its intensity

He'd enjoyed her company. Her words, her laughter, her energy made him feel good. If only he could spend time with her again, to store up the ease and electricity he felt when he was with her. But he couldn't see her again. It wasn't fair to her. She should be with someone who wanted a baby as badly as she did.

He shoved a hand through his hair and wondered if he should get it cut. Groaning, he gave up any pretense of getting work done, picked up his phone and called Tim, a fellow rancher he'd become friends with. His friend answered on the third ring.

"Hey, Sander, how's it going?"

"It's a little crazy right now." He looked around his office, wondering how his life had gone so off-kilter.

"Tell me about it," Tim said. "With the holidays and Cheryl's family coming in and the kids' school activities—I don't remember ever being this busy."

"Any chance you want to take a break and grab a beer?"

His friend groaned. "I'd love to, but I'm pretty sure Cheryl will have my head if I put anything else on the calendar. How about we catch up after the first of the year."

He called his friend Jack next.

"Sorry, buddy, but we're headed out for a family trip to Disney. I'll let you know when I'm back."

"Damn, it never used to be this hard to hang out with you and the gang," Sander said.

Jack laughed. "I think you're remembering wrong, old friend. You were always busy with the kids."

"I guess you're right," Sander said, shaking his head. "I missed a lot of bonfires and bar crawls back in the day."

His call to his other friend Stuart went straight to voicemail.

He sighed. Now that he was finally free, his buddies weren't.

He was too restless to sit at his desk and too distracted to focus on architectural plans. Changing into jeans and boots, he grabbed his Stetson and headed to Walsh's Equestrian Estate. Maybe a ride in the temperate December weather would clear his mind and put him in a better mood.

His phone rang, and he let Kesley's call go to voicemail. A twinge of guilt stabbed him, but he didn't want to answer her giddy questions about last night's date. Because deep down he didn't want to admit that his heart was a little sore from opening up to the possibility of falling for someone, only to realize he and Lisa weren't a match. He'd get over it—eventually—but he wanted a little more time.

He parked his truck at the equestrian center, rolled his shoulders, and remembered another conversation he and Kelsey had a few weeks ago. She'd run into Aaron Walsh, who'd told her he'd seen someone arguing with Linc shortly before the kid was murdered. His chest ached at the memory. Even though Linc had been killed five months ago, the pain was still fresh, especially since the killer had yet to be found. The anger he felt at the injustice of it all still burned.

Blowing out a breath, Sander jammed his Stetson on his head. If Aaron was around, he'd gauge his mood, see if he knew any more details about this person he'd spotted getting into it with Linc. Not that he was a detective or anything, but as a de facto dad to the kid, responsibility weighed heavy on him. He still woke up in a cold sweat, wondering what happened. Maybe if he talked to Aaron, it would help him feel like he was doing *something*.

Stepping out of his truck, he inhaled the odors of horse, hay, and manure. Despite his preference for the behind-a-desk side of things, those horse smells were almost a part of his DNA. No matter how crazy life and clients and kids might get, the second he absorbed those scents, his heartbeat slowed, his breathing evened out, and life seemed more bearable.

He headed toward the stable. The Mediterranean-style building sat on fifty acres, with stucco exteriors and red slate roofs. With Christmas around the corner, it was decorated with pine boughs, like almost everything in Emerald Ridge. As he entered, horses whinnied and bits jangled. His boots clopped on the cement floors, muffled slightly by sawdust. He peeked his head into the main office, but it was deserted. Aaron was nowhere to be seen.

"Howdy, Mr. Fortune. Can I help you?" A young stable hand he'd seen many times before raced up to him, a grin on his freckled face, his body slightly awkward.

"Tommy, right?"

The guy nodded eagerly. "That's me! You want to ride today?"

"I thought I'd saddle up Sand Dollar and take her out for a ride."

Tommy's face creased in confusion. "You don't need to saddle him up, Mr. Fortune. That's my job."

"Oh, that's right. Sorry about that." As he walked with Tommy toward Sand Dollar's stall, Sander berated himself for forgetting how literal the young man was.

Nodding, Tommy led the sorrel out of the stall, attached him to leads connected to the wall, and heaved a saddle blanket over his back. Then, without another word, the stable hand left, returning after just a few seconds later with Sander's saddle. Once he'd tightened the girth around the horse's stomach and attached the bridle, he handed the reins over to Sander.

"Here you go, Mr. Fortune."

"Thanks, Tommy." He looked around the quiet stable. "Not many riders today?"

Tommy shook his head. "We were busier over the weekend." He stood at Sand Dollar's head, patting his nose. "A couple tourists took Linc's horse out on Sunday." His face brightened. "I was glad to see her get some exercise."

Sander felt a pang of guilt. He hadn't ridden Linc's horse in months. "I'm glad she's getting the attention she needs."

Tommy pursed his lips. "I miss him a lot. He was always nice to me."

"I miss him, too, buddy." Sander swallowed, trying

to force air into his lungs, which were suddenly tight. For all his troubles, Linc had been a decent kid.

Sander looked around, searching for something—*anything*—to make the pain of losing Linc lessen. And then his gaze landed on Tommy, the gangly man with mussed hair who said exactly what he meant. The guy had a way with horses, even if he didn't always understand people. And yet, Linc had made an impression on him. Sander's chest eased and a hint of the peace he was searching for washed over him. Tommy had liked Linc.

Sander was about to lead the horse out of the stable, when Tommy continued. "I can't believe Linc was murdered. Doesn't seem right." The stable hand pursed his lips, making circles in the sawdust with the toe of his boot. "He was right here a day or two before he was killed, chatting with Aaron like everything was perfectly normal. Gosh, life changes so fast." Tommy's face drooped with sorrow, his gaze somewhere off in the distance.

Sander turned in the entryway of the stable. "He was? Are you sure?"

Tommy nodded his head, taking the reins from Sander and leading Sand Dollar outside to the mounting block. "Aaron said Linc was interested in buying a few more horses. I guess he thought Linc's horse needed some friends."

Hmm. Aaron hadn't mentioned seeing Linc right before he was killed, even while telling Kelsey about someone arguing with Linc in a park. Wouldn't he *also* have added seeing him in the stable? The two sightings went together. At least they did to Sander.

"You know, Tommy, you should tell the police what you saw."

Tommy swung around. "I should? Why?"

"Because it might be important in their investigation. They might want to talk to Aaron about it."

Tommy frowned. "But people talk to Aaron all the time about buying horses."

"Yes, but how many of those people are murdered?"

Tommy's eyes widened and his mouth dropped open. "You don't think Aaron is in danger, do you? Maybe I should warn him."

That was the last thing they needed, someone shooting off their mouth about every observation they had. "Hold on, Tommy. I don't think he's in any danger. And I wouldn't tell anyone but the police what you saw or heard, not even Aaron."

"Oh, I don't know, Mr. Fortune. He's my boss. Doesn't seem right to keep something this important from him. What if something *did* happen to him? If I'd kept my mouth shut, I'd feel just awful."

Sander adjusted the reins in his hands. The poor guy was obviously conflicted, and Sander felt for him. But this was murder they were talking about, and after five months, it didn't seem as if the police knew anything. Maybe Tommy's recollection would help them. "It's up to you, Tommy. But I'd hate for Aaron to get upset with you, thinking you were snooping on his private conversations."

Tommy's face reddened. "Shoot, I wasn't snooping.

But I'd hate for Aaron to get angry at me, Mr. Fortune." He blew out a breath. "I…uh… won't say anything except to the police."

"Smart move, Tommy. I'll see you later." Tipping his hat at the young man, he squeezed Sand Dollar's flanks, then headed toward the open pasture.

As he galloped through the tall fescue and orchard fields, the wind ruffled his hair at his collar, and the tangy smell of the grass mixed with horse sweat. He'd made this ride hundreds of times, probably thousands. But unlike all the other times when it had cleared his head, this time it didn't. With every clop of the hooves, his conversation with Tommy echoed through his head, growing louder the farther from the stables he traveled. Nothing made sense.

He groaned. It was times like these that he missed his brother, Mark. Older than him by eighteen years, he'd been more like an extra father figure than brother. He'd disciplined him almost as much as his parents while growing up. Sander still remembered the disappointment on all their faces, even Mark's, when he first told them Lani was pregnant. Bile burned in his stomach. He'd shouldered his responsibility immediately, and thankfully their disappointment had transformed to pride.

He liked to think his brother would have turned into more of a friend later in life and been able to provide him with advice. Or at least serve as a sounding board for all of his questions. Like Lisa.

He jerked in his saddle, pulling the reins hard

enough that Sand Dollar stumbled before righting himself and slowing to a trot.

He patted the horse's neck. "Sorry about that," he said softly.

Talking to Lisa last night had been so easy. God, he could just picture being with a woman like her, where the two of them could be comfortable talking about everything. How she'd listen with that small furrow between her eyebrows, focused solely on him. He imagined the wheels in her mind spinning out solutions, solutions that made sense. Her intelligence had drawn him in last night. His shoulders slumped with disappointment over the futility of pursuing a romance with her, because he suspected they'd be great together.

He stewed, wondering about what could have been, and missing the chance to talk out his problems with her. Heck, he'd missed out on the chance to be a good listener to her, too, since her conversation about babies had spooked him so much. Regret washed over him. She'd deserved someone to listen to her problems just as much as he did.

He'd let her down.

Sander kicked the horse's sides to continue their gallop, needing the breeze against his face to blow away the guilt weighing him down. *He* was the responsible one. The one who was always there for everyone when they needed him. And he hadn't been there, not fully, for Lisa. The muffled clop of Sand Dollar's hooves seemed to echo "you failed" as he rode, and he shook his head.

No, he hadn't failed. No matter how great he and

Lisa were together, their dreams didn't match. And no one should have to give up what mattered most to be with another person. That was the one thing he was sure of. But just because they couldn't be together as a couple, didn't mean they couldn't be friends. His pulse quickened at the idea. He could be a good friend, listen to her problems, and hopefully make up for letting her down before. It couldn't hurt to ask.

With newfound intent and a clearer head, Sander turned Sand Dollar around and headed back to the stable. Once inside, he dismounted and led the horse back to his stall. A tall blond man in the distance grabbed his attention.

"Hey, Finn," he called out to the young guy. His niece Zara had dated Finn Morrison when they were teenagers, but something had happened between the two of them, and they had parted ways. It was too bad. He'd liked the guy a lot. And Zara was still suffering from a broken heart.

Finn glanced over at him, his expression troubled. Maybe Finn was suffering too. "Hey," he said, raising a hand.

Sander finished unsaddling Sand Dollar and nodded to Tommy to take over. Concerned, he walked over to Finn.

"You doin' okay?"

Finn exhaled, fisting his hands at his sides. He was silent for a few seconds. Was he hesitant to talk to Sander because of his relationship with Zara? Sander was about to press him, to reassure him that he could be an impartial listener, when Finn spoke. "I'm guessing you know about the birth file Kelsey and Priscilla found on Linc's houseboat?"

Sander's eyes widened in momentary surprise at the turn in conversation, but nodded. His daughter and his other niece had found the file in a secret drawer beneath Linc's bed in the houseboat Priscilla had inherited after Linc's death. Because Finn's name was on it, they'd handed the manila folder over to him. Everyone was dying to know what was inside it, but, so far, the guy had remained mum.

"I do. Have you taken a look at it?"

Finn shook his head, eyes tormented. "I wish they hadn't found that damn file." He huffed out a breath. "I can't stop thinking about it, but I'm afraid if I open it, I'll find out something I wish I didn't know. Yet I'm curious too." He shook his head and groaned.

Sander's heart bled for the guy. "I'm sorry. That's gotta be rough. Listen, those adoption records have been around for years. They can wait a little longer. Don't rush anything. You'll know when the time is right." No matter how curious he was about its contents.

"If it ever is," Finn muttered.

He met the man's gaze and gave him a reassuring nod. "And if it isn't, that's okay too. Sometimes, ignorance is bliss. No one can make you ready, though, but you."

Finn patted his horse's neck. "You're right. I just can't decide if knowing the file exists is worse than getting my questions answered. Like how the heck *my* parents, who had absolutely no money, could afford

Texas Royale Private Adoption Agency. Do you have any idea how expensive that place is?"

Sander had wondered about that too. "Yeah, it's strange the agency chose them as your adoptive parents." He held up a hand. "I know that sounds harsh. I don't mean any offense. Your parents were wonderful, and money, or lack thereof, shouldn't determine who gets to be a parent." He remembered Lisa's conversation about how expensive IVF was, and Sander realized, despite everything, how lucky he was to have gotten the chance to raise kids. Lisa would make a great mom. He hoped she'd be able to become one despite the obstacles she was facing.

Finn nodded. "I know. None taken. It's just one more mystery. And as much as I'm dragging my feet, I'd like some answers…and closure."

"Just take your time. One way or another, everything will come out in due time."

Finn exhaled. "I hope so."

The fatherly side of Sander reared its head. Maybe it was all the talk about babies. "Have you been in touch with Zara?" Sander asked, trying to change the subject and satisfy his own curiosity.

Finn's face clouded. "No, we seem to be avoiding each other." He shrugged.

But somehow, Sander read more in that one shrug than he suspected Finn wanted to show. The man was hurting, and if Sander had to guess, at least as much as his niece was.

"That's too bad," he said. Zara and Finn had been good together back in high school. He hoped they'd reconnect and get a second chance. Finn was a great guy, and he'd been good for Zara.

Patting the man on the back, Sander left the stable, more conflicted than ever. Linc, Aaron, Finn. There were too many variables and nothing made sense. His chest burned with the need to talk to someone, but who was he supposed to turn to? His family? He couldn't burden them with all this. They had enough on their minds. Kelsey had Trevor's triplets to deal with. His nieces and nephews, and Kelsey, too, were still reeling over Linc's murder. It was his responsibility to help them, not add to their troubles.

Lisa.

She popped into his head like a beacon of light, and he couldn't tear his thoughts away. Their conversation last night had flowed so easily. She was smart and rational, and he'd just bet he'd feel better after talking to her. He shook his head and climbed into his truck. Pounding the steering wheel in frustration, he let out a groan before shaking out his hand to relieve the sting.

He couldn't ask her for help when she'd ended their date so abruptly. Calling her at the first sign of trouble, after the way he'd left things last night, wasn't fair. If he was going to make the first move toward friendship, he had to show her he could listen to her too.

So maybe his first step was to apologize and then see if they could be friends. And why would she want to hear from him? Hell, as soon as she'd found out he wasn't interested in having any more children, she'd practically run out of the restaurant. He didn't blame her. He'd basically dashed any hope of a relationship with her.

Unless.

Unless he called to apologize. Maybe she really would want to be friends. Maybe the idea would appeal to her as much as it did to him.

Before he could convince himself otherwise, he dialed her number as he walked to his truck. Her voice made his spine tingle.

"I can't stop thinking about you," he said. *Whoa.* He hadn't meant to say that. He cleared his throat. "I'm sorry, that probably makes me sound like a creep." Sander stared off into the distance. So much for friendship.

"I'm having the same problem," she answered softly.

Her response stopped him mid-step, causing his chest to tighten with excitement.

"I didn't expect that response," he admitted.

"I didn't expect your phone call."

He leaned against the door of his truck, kicking the small white stones with the tip of his boot. "Maybe we should do something about this…um…our inability to stop thinking about each other." Seriously, when was the last time anyone made him act like this? Lines and planes—that's what he understood. But women? Clearly not. Thank God she couldn't see him.

Lisa's sigh echoed in his ear. "Sander, we're not meant to be. I want children. You don't. That's a chasm that can't be crossed. We're too old to force a relationship."

"Ouch. We're not *that* old."

She laughed, making him smile just...because. "Maybe you're not," she conceded. "But my students think I'm ancient. And my biological clock is ticking." She whispered the last part, and his heart ached for her.

"What about friends?" he asked. "Couldn't we be that?" That was the reason he'd called, even if his traitorous tongue formed definitely-not-friends words.

Lisa's pause was so long, sweat popped on the back of his neck. Had he misread the situation? Did she not enjoy their dinner as much as he had? Maybe she was only interested in a potential husband.

"I think I'd like that," she whispered.

The muscles in his neck relaxed. "Good." He couldn't help the grin that stretched his cheeks. "I would too." He paused and cleared his throat. "So, uh, now what?" *God, the Genius Bar had nothing on me.* He shut his eyes. Lines and planes.

Her throaty laughter made him think maybe he hadn't embarrassed himself too much. Or if he had, she enjoyed it. "I seem to recall offering to teach you to bake rugelach," she said. "Any interest in coming over later to learn?"

Baking had never been his thing, but suddenly, an afternoon in the kitchen with Lisa sounded like the best idea he'd heard in a long time.

"I'd like that. What can I bring?"

"Just yourself."

Chapter Five

His mama hadn't raised him to show up empty-handed, so he'd have to stop somewhere to pick up something before he went to her house. Agreeing to see her later, he drove home to shower off the horse smell and change into something that didn't look like he'd just been in a barn. Which he had. Feeling better than he had all day, he whistled to himself as he got ready, shoved his Stetson on his head, and drove to Emerald Ridge Floral. He'd pick up a bouquet of flowers and a bottle of wine. Did rugelach go with white or red? He frowned, deciding instead to pick up a Leonetti dessert wine. In the flower section, he avoided the roses—the two of them were just friends—and instead, grabbed a bouquet of daisies and lilies. The bright colors reminded him of her smile—joyful. He paid the clerk and headed to Lisa's house.

On his way, he remembered Kelsey's call that he'd ignored, and punched her number into his phone.

"Hey, sweetie, what's up?" He didn't hear the triplets in the background, which probably meant she was at work on her ranch. Maybe she wanted help with the ranch.

"I wanted a debrief on last night's date."

Debrief. Of course. He chuckled. "It...didn't go great."

"Oh, I'm sorry. Wait, why are you laughing? Oh my God, was it *that* bad? Did the restaurant kick you two out or something?" She moaned loudly. "Darn it, I wanted to go there with Trevor for his birthday, but if you got yourselves kicked out, they'll never let a Fortune in again."

"Kels, relax, we didn't get kicked out."

"Then why was it bad?"

"We have different goals." He wasn't about to tell her, at least not right now, specifically how those goals differed.

She sighed. "Well, it's *her* loss. Want to come over for dinner?"

Sander warmed at his daughter's loyalty and devotion. "Actually, I'm headed over to her place right now, but rain check?"

"But I thought—"

"We didn't click romantically—" there was no way he was talking about their chemistry to his daughter "—but we did platonically. So we agreed to be friends."

"Oh. Um. Huh. Well, that's nice. If you're sure..."

"I am, sweetheart, but thank you for the invitation, say hi to Trevor and hug those triplets for me."

He disconnected the call as he pulled onto Lisa's street. Located in a quiet residential part of Emerald Ridge, her house was a small, single-family home with a whitewashed brick exterior. Most of the homes in the neighborhood were decorated for Christmas with inflatable snowmen or Santas in front yards, lights outlining the peaks of the roofs, and wreaths on the front doors. Lisa's was bare, save for an electric menorah in the front window.

As he pulled into the driveway, he could picture her with a bunch of kids and a husband living here. Well, maybe not a *bunch*, because the home was tiny. At least, that's how it looked from the outside. It was situated in the perfect neighborhood with sidewalks, one where he'd expect youngsters on bikes to ride after school and on weekends, to play wiffle ball and climb trees and sell homemade lemonade. He shook his head. Talk about fantasy life. Did kids even play outside anymore? Most he knew liked to sit indoors with headphones on, playing video games on their devices. Still, it had the possibility of being the perfect neighborhood *if* children wanted to romp outdoors. He paused. Had she and her husband pictured that as well when they purchased it? Had they walked around the yard, pointing out the location of a swing set? Wandered down the block, wondering which homes would house their kids' best friends? He shook his head, pushing away any thoughts about her previous life. Didn't matter what they'd done back then. Life had turned out different. For both of them.

He rang the bell and a moment later she answered. Her curly brown hair was caught in a messy bun on the top of her head, a few strands loose around her face. His eyes drifted lower. Her cleavage was on full display in a deep V-neck, long-sleeved pink top, and he'd never seen anyone wear a pair of jeans the way she did. He swallowed. His hands itched to take her in his arms and admire her body with his lips, but they were friends. Friends didn't do that, and certainly not in the way his libido was suggesting to him.

"Hi." She swung the black door wide and ushered him inside her entryway. It was a little cramped, but would have enough room for a pair or two of shoes or boots and an umbrella. "Come on inside."

He stepped over the threshold and, oddly nervous, handed her the flowers and wine he'd brought, hoping she'd like them. "These are for you."

She flushed with pleasure. "Sander, these are gorgeous. Thank you. Make yourself comfortable and I'll put the flowers in water and the wine in the fridge."

She led him into the living room, an open and airy room with lots of windows, a brick fireplace, and colorful art on the walls. The space was decorated for Hanukkah, with dreidels on the mantel and the candelabra he'd seen from the street sat in the window.

"Have a seat," she said, gesturing toward the sectional as she proceeded into the kitchen. "Can I get you a drink? Wine, beer, soda?" she asked as she filled a vase with water and placed the flowers in it.

"A beer would be great," he replied, sinking into the pewter-colored sectional. With his long legs, most sofas weren't particularly comfortable, but this one was. He looked around the room while Lisa was off getting drinks, his architectural eye taking everything in. Warm-hued tones, a variety of fabric textures, and pops of color on the walls made it an inviting place to be. It suited her. Still, the hard surfaces would cause children's voices to echo louder than usual. If it were his home, he'd add more built-ins for storage. Kids needed *lots* of storage.

"Here you go." She handed him a bottle of Shiner Bock, and he grinned.

"You stock good beer."

"It's a Texas favorite." She raised her own bottle to his and tapped it lightly. "To friendship."

"To friendship." He swallowed the slightly sweet, nutty, caramel flavor before resting the bottle on his knee. "I was just thinking how this room suits you," he said.

"Really?" She folded her legs under her and turned sideways to face him. "Why?"

"Warm, colorful, and real. No pretense."

She smiled. "Thank you. My mom and sister helped me decorate it, but the style definitely suits me."

"I owe you an apology," he said, unable to hold back for the right moment. He'd meant to apologize when they were on the phone, but their conversation had ended before he had a chance. Even though he didn't want to dampen the mood, he needed their friendship to start with a clean slate. "I ended our night kind of abruptly, and that was wrong of me. I'm sorry."

"I'm the one who rushed out. We were on a date, and we're old enough to know when something isn't going to work. You were honest, something I appreciate. There's no use trying to force it."

"Still, I should have shown better manners. Maybe been a little less blunt. I'll try to do better."

"And I shouldn't have been so quick to run off." She winked, and he couldn't help but chuckle. "Speaking of friends, or maybe I should say *as* friends, you look stressed."

He startled. She barely knew him, yet she could tell? "I didn't know I was that obvious," he said.

"I'm a teacher of middle school students. Part of my job is recognizing the outward signs of inner turmoil."

"You're very good at it."

She settled back into the cushions and fixed him with her gaze. "So does that mean I'm right?"

He nodded and took another gulp of his beer.

"Well, I'm a good listener if you want to talk…"

He'd wanted to talk to her about Linc. After all, she was the first person to pop into his mind when he realized he needed another opinion, he reminded himself. But faced with the opportunity, the words suddenly stuck in his throat. He gripped his bottle of beer tighter. "I do, but I need you to understand that what I tell you can't go any further than this room."

"As long as you're not about to confess to a crime, you can count on my secrecy," she said. Her tone was light, but her expression grew serious. "You're *not*, right?"

He shook his head. "No, but it does relate to Linc Banning's death, I think. Or maybe not. I'm not sure."

Placing her bottle of beer on the coffee table, she leaned forward. "That explains your turmoil. I'm very good at keeping things to myself, so you have nothing to worry about from me."

Taking a deep breath, he told her everything that had happened since Linc's murder. "Kelsey and Priscilla think maybe Linc planned to sell the adoption records to Finn, but for some reason, backed out of the agreement and hid Finn's records in the secret drawer in his houseboat." He wrung his hands. "I don't know, maybe there was something painful in them that he didn't think Finn could handle. Or maybe he didn't think anyone should know. But now Finn's afraid to look at them, which I understand, but I just wish he'd read them so we'd all get some answers."

"Wow." Lisa shook her head. "Just, wow. Now I understand why you look stressed." Her expression softened as she looked at him.

He'd been right. Opening up to her made him feel better. "And I can't talk to my family about this. They've all got their own problems and don't need to deal with anything else. Nor do I want anyone gossiping about it. It's hard enough on Finn and everyone else involved without their thinking that people are whispering behind their backs." He scrubbed a hand across his jaw. "I just wish Linc had felt able to confide in me. I could have helped him." His chest ached with all the might-have-beens.

"Of course you would have."

Her confidence bolstered him. "So you see why I said you can't tell anyone."

She nodded. "I do. And I promise to keep it all to myself." She turned, staring out the window at the afternoon light that was already beginning to fade. The sun reflected off the neck of the beer bottle, casting her skin in an amber glow.

It took Sander's breath away.

"You know, I can understand why Linc might have felt an affinity for Finn," she continued.

Sander waited her out. He'd learned in their short time together that she was careful with her words, thinking before speaking, and that when she *did* say something, it made a lot of sense. But when the silence stretched a shade too long, his curiosity got the better of him.

"Why?" He gripped the beer bottle tight and stared at her.

She bit her lip. "The two of them came from similar backgrounds. Neither was born into a wealthy family, and both have been drawn into the fold to some extent. And that's hard."

Sander frowned. "We've never used our money as a barrier between anyone. None of us judge people by their wealth, and we are all welcoming to everyone."

"That may be true," she acknowledged. "And I'm not criticizing you or your family. But no matter how inclusive you are, someone who comes from the kind of wealth that you do can't possibly understand what it's like to have none. And so I would think that when Linc and Finn met, there was a sigh of relief, if only from the standpoint that the two of them were standing on the same footing. They didn't need to pretend or make allowances or excuses around each other. They could just *be*."

Sander leaned against the sofa cushion, contemplating Lisa's words. Could she be right? He thought back to when Linc and his mom had joined their family. He'd required a housekeeper to help with the five kids, and Delia had needed a job and a safe place for her son. In his mind, it had been an even bargain. He'd included them in all family activities, never making it seem like they were the hired help.

But maybe in their minds it had been different, especially since he paid her salary.

He remembered holiday celebrations. Sander had always bought gifts, but Delia and Linc had usually made theirs. He'd always admired the work, thinking they were even more meaningful because they'd spent time putting them together. He'd never judged or placed less of a value on them, but had *they*? And when he complained one day about how fast the kids were growing and their need for new clothes, Delia had laughed in commiseration. Yet she'd happily taken the boys' old clothes and given them to Linc, rather than buy new ones.

Linc had been a quiet kid, joining in with the others in whatever activity they were involved in, but at the same time, always seeming to hold back. When Finn had come along, dating Zara during the Fortune's summer vacations in Emerald Ridge, Sander had seen the boy blossom, coming out of his shell for the first time. He'd never thought much of it. But maybe Lisa was right. He wished he could talk to Delia about whether they'd ever felt out of place, although he had a sneaking suspicion her pride wouldn't allow her to tell him the whole truth.

He shook his head. "I never thought of it that way," he finally said. "Which probably just means I do take my family's wealth for granted."

Lisa put her hand on his leg. He wanted to cover it with his own, but he refrained.

"No," she said gently, "it means that's all you've

ever known. You're a good man. I doubt anything you did or didn't do caused Linc any more discomfort. It's just the way things are."

"You seem to know a lot about this. Do I make you uncomfortable too?"

Her amber eyes widened, lashes long. God, she was beautiful.

"Absolutely not," she said. "In fact, you made me more comfortable when we had dinner than I thought I'd be." Her cheeks reddened, giving her face a rosy hue. He wanted to cup her cheeks and bask in her warmth.

He had to stop thinking of her that way.

"I'd wondered what it would be like, going out on a date with such a wealthy man," she added. "But once we started talking, I forgot about your money and your background, at least for a little while."

"And now? Is my name an impediment to our being friends?"

"No." She took another sip of her beer, her lips closing around the bottle.

He shifted his seat, his attraction for her intensifying.

We're just friends. Our last date proved that.

Still, he couldn't help staring at her mouth, wishing he could taste her.

She placed her beer bottle on the table. "Ready for your rugelach lesson?"

His attention snapped back to their planned activity. *Rugelach. Right.* "Will it be as fun as the last one?"

She winked. "I don't know. You'll have to tell me afterward."

He followed her into the small but well-appointed

kitchen. A round table sat on one end, up against a counter island that separated the eating area from the breakfast nook. The windows overlooked the backyard. If this were his kitchen, he'd bump out the back...

It wasn't his kitchen. He had to stop looking at everything with his architect's eye. He washed his hands at the sink. As Lisa pulled out the ingredients for their lesson, he sat on a stool at the counter examining the items and wondering how exactly they'd all go together.

"Would you like one?" She held out an apron with *Happy Hanukkah* stitched in blue and yellow, and then wrapped a matching one around her waist.

"Is this your way of telling me I'm a slob?"

"Do you want to risk it?"

He laughed. "Probably not, if only because if I don't wear it, I'll spill."

"Yeah, better safe than sorry. It would be shame to mess up that shirt. It looks good on you."

She paused, and in the silence, he thought he noticed a flash of heat in her eyes. The gold flecks sparkled for a brief second before she blinked, and anything he thought he saw disappeared.

"Thank you."

They began measuring and mixing ingredients, forming the dough into balls.

"While they cool in the fridge, how about we order dinner?" Lisa asked.

Sander's stomach growled just at that moment, making her laugh. "I'll take that as a yes."

"Probably a good idea," he said. "You haven't seen me when I'm hungry."

"Oh, are you one of those hangry people?"

"I can be." He grimaced, just for fun. "You?"

She let out another laugh. "You think I'm going to tell you that?"

He tapped the countertop. "Come on, we're friends, aren't we? Friends tell each other things."

"Then I guess as your *friend*, I should tell you that you have flour on your face." Her eyes glinted with merriment.

He jerked. "I do?" He wiped his cheek, but she shook her head.

"Nope, not there."

"Where?"

He wiped his other cheek.

"Still not there." This time, she walked around the counter. Her warm vanilla scent, which tickled his nostrils, sent his senses into high alert. Seated on the stool, his knees pressed against her jeans-clad thighs as she leaned close to him. The V of her top gave him another peek at her cleavage. Then she brushed his nose, and an electric charge leaped from her fingers to his body, sending streaks of red-hot desire along his spine. He gazed into her eyes, and their liquid heat drew him in. Her incredibly long lashes fluttered. When she bit her bottom lip, he stifled a groan.

"Lisa," he whispered.

She slid her hands along his cheeks, reminding him of what he'd wanted to do to her. Her skin was so soft, he wanted to take her hands in his mouth. Instead, he reached for her, running his hands along her ribs to her waist before pulling her close. She stepped between his knees. Her mouth was mere inches away, and his breath hitched. Unable to look at anything but her mouth, he swallowed. Her lips were full and pink and he had to taste them.

She licked her bottom lip and ran her hands through his hair. He wanted to moan with pleasure.

"What are we doing?" he asked, barely in control of himself.

"I hope you're going to kiss me."

"But we're friends." He ground out the words, hating every syllable but not wanting to hurt her.

"Can we be friends who kiss?"

The question sent a shock of longing through him, and he cupped her cheeks and finally joined his mouth to hers. She tasted as good as she smelled. His body hummed as he devoured her mouth, her tongue swiping inside and tussling with his. She wrapped her arms around his neck and whimpered as their kiss deepened. Her breasts pressed against his chest, and he dropped his hands to her sides as he rose off the stool and stood before her. He slid his fingers beneath the hem of her shirt, teasing her soft skin with his fingertips, and he hardened against her. His need for her overwhelming him. And then she was unbuttoning his shirt, and a shred of reality pierced his lustful haze. He broke the seal of their kiss for a moment.

"Lisa," he rasped, his voice gravelly with need. "Tell me what you want."

"I want you," she said, sliding her hands around his waist and beneath his shirt.

"But—"

She pressed her finger against his lips to shush him. "I want you," she repeated.

That was all he needed to hear. He lifted her shirt over her head, and his breath caught at the sight of her breasts straining against the lace of her bra. His blood rushed south, and he focused on maintaining control as her breathing grew harsh. Standing on tiptoe, she pushed his shirt over his shoulders, before licking every inch of his chest with her tongue.

In turn, he lowered his head and feathered kisses across her collarbone, grabbing her bra strap with his teeth and moving it off her shoulder. Her skin pebbled into goose bumps beneath him, and he smiled against her as he continued his trail down to her breast, taking first one nipple and then the other between his lips. She hissed as he grazed them with his teeth. His hands lowered to her waist, and he caressed her with his thumbs, loving the texture of her.

"Sander," she moaned.

Pulling away, he watched her head fall back, exposing the arch of her neck. His nerves hummed as he rose and kissed his way back until he reached her ear, which he nibbled as her pulse throbbed against his chin. He thrust his hands into her hair. The thick curls tickled his fingers, their silky softness driving him mad. They were even softer than he'd imagined. God, he wanted this woman. But they were supposed to be just friends.

Through the thick haze of his desire, a slice of anxiety cut through. He didn't want to lead her on or do anything to hurt her. Kissing was one thing. But where they were headed...

"Lisa," he said.

"I love how you say my name." She closed her eyes and pressed against him, making it impossible for him to think. But he had to.

He pulled away. "Wait."

She blinked her eyes open, eyes that were dark with desire. For him.

He swallowed. "I want you," he gritted out, "but I don't want to hurt you."

Her gaze softened. "I want you too." She took his hand and pulled him toward the door to a hallway he hadn't seen.

"Are you sure?"

It would take everything he had to turn away from her, but he'd do it to protect her.

"More than sure," she said.

He followed her, entranced by the sway of her hips as she led him down a short hallway to her bedroom. At least, he assumed it was her bedroom. His attention was solely focused on her. They could have been on Mars for all he knew. But Mars didn't smell like honeysuckle. And Mars didn't have a silky bed to lean against as he took her in his arms and once again, kissed her senseless.

When he finally pulled away from her luscious mouth, she leaned her forehead against his shoulder and unbuttoned his jeans. He throbbed against the zipper and hissed when she finally released him. Shucking his pants and his boots as fast as his trembling hands could manage, he stood before her almost naked.

* * *

Oh my God, Sander Fortune was in her bedroom. Almost naked. Looking at her the way people normally looked at the desserts she baked—like he couldn't wait to devour her.

Lisa's heart pounded against her ribs and tremors ran through her body. Every nerve ending burned. Her knees trembled, and her fingertips actually itched to touch him everywhere. Like the way they did when the challah dough dried on her skin and she had to scrub her hands under hot water to get all of it off.

Hmm, she wouldn't mind scrubbing him under water.

She shook her head to clear it, took a step forward, and reached for him. Taut abs, light dusting of hair, powerful shoulders, trim waist. Her mouth watered as she traced the outlines of his muscles. His gaze pierced hers, locked on her, pupils dilated. And as she moved her hands across his chest, his breath hitched, echoing around them, and he clenched his hands into fists at his sides.

Why wasn't he touching her? The more she stroked him, the more she wanted his skin against hers, his hands around her waist. Or better yet, on her breasts. She rose on tiptoe and took his earlobe in her mouth. He groaned.

The sound made her shiver. Finally, he reached for her and pulled her against him. Now their bare chests touched, and the contact set her skin on fire. She gasped as he reached for her mouth, covering it with his. Their hot breaths mingled once again and all clear thought vanished in a haze of desire.

"You're so beautiful," he whispered, as he backed her up against her bed. They tumbled onto the quilt, the throw pillows bouncing.

She swept her hand to the side, tossing them onto the floor. He wrapped his arms around her, knotting his fingers in her hair, devouring every inch of skin until she swore she'd go up in flames.

"I want you," she mouthed against his ear.

He licked his way down her body, making her tremble with need. When he returned to her mouth, his eyes gleamed. "I want you too."

She rose, leaned over to the night table and pulled out a condom from the drawer. His eyes widened as she tore the foil packet with her teeth, then rose up on her knees and pushed him against the pillows. As she rolled it over him, he shut his eyes tight, hissing once again at the contact. When she was finished, he pulled her beneath him, using his hands and mouth to get her ready. She was moaning after only a few minutes, needing him inside her.

"Please," she whispered, staring into his eyes. Golden flecks made them glow, reminding her of flames. Just like the flames that heated her body. When she thought she could stand it no longer, he held himself over her, supported by muscular arms, and lowered himself into her. She sighed in relief, until desire overwhelmed her. He moved slowly, and her body welcomed him, clenching around him and making him grunt. His skin was firm and slightly rough beneath her palms, his muscles hard, adding texture, strength, and power. They moved together as one, finding their rhythm. His pupils dilated and his breath came in harsh bursts, his face taut and controlled.

Every move she made, every stroke brought out a reaction in him, giving her power and control. Finally, when she didn't think she could stand it anymore, he seated himself fully inside her, filling her and making her muscles stretch with a delicious pull. They rocked together, faster and longer, until she lost track of everything but the deep need for release. Her vision blurred, her pulse pounded in her ears and, with a scream, she toppled over the edge. She shuddered, her muscles spasming, while streaks of heat continued to run through her. His skin dampened, his breaths bellowed, and with a last shout, he collapsed on top of her.

They cocooned together as they recovered, limbs wrapped around each other, hearts beating in tandem. He stroked her back, and she ran her foot along his leg. Finally, she opened her eyes. He watched her, his eyes molten, lines splaying from their corners. She raised a hand and traced those lines, before running her hands through his hair, damp with sweat.

"Thank you," he said, his gravelly voice pitched low.

She'd never had a man thank her for sex before. "I could say the same to you." Her mouth stretched in a lazy grin.

"No, not for that, although that was fantastic. But thank you for the condom. I know how much you want a child, and it means a lot that you gave it to me without hesitation."

She angled up on one arm, a slash of nausea running through her. "I'd be a pretty awful person if I hadn't. I don't go around trapping men into making me a mom, even if it *were* possible for me to get pregnant."

He caressed her face. "It never even occurred to me that you would. I was simply commenting on the ease with which you took care of it."

The irritation that had started, lessened. While she'd never be the kind of person to trick someone, she'd heard stories of those who did. And being a Fortune, maybe more people tried to do that to him.

She nodded.

"You're a good person," he said tenderly. "I admire your strength and your honesty."

A part of her didn't want to be admired. It was too distancing, and what she wanted most was to belong. But another part of her was proud of the very traits he admired, and was glad to have found someone who valued them, even if they couldn't be together. She turned her head, burying it in the crook of his arm. Wishing and hoping for things she couldn't have hadn't gotten her anywhere. She was going to appreciate what she currently had and not worry about the future.

"Thank you."

She snuggled up against him, and they drifted off to sleep, waking up together a little more than an hour later. Opening her eyes and seeing him sleeping next to her brought home everything they'd just done. A million emotions ran through her.

He was the first man after her husband that she'd slept with. At first, she hadn't been interested in anyone. And then she'd been scared. Afraid of forgetting Jordan, or comparing someone new to him. But with Sander, she hadn't been scared. She hadn't thought of anyone or anything at all. Passion had built and the sex had felt completely natural between the two of them

She sucked in a quick breath of amazement, thinking about how wonderful their encounter had been. Her body flooded with renewed desire as she remained wrapped in his arms. Despite not knowing him long, she was at ease with him. Yet, the longer she lay there, the tighter the knot in her belly grew.

Because, despite how much they both enjoyed each other, how combustible they were in the bedroom, they'd decided to be friends.

Friends with benefits? She wasn't sure she liked that idea. But then again, she didn't think she was completely against it. The thought of having to cut him out of her life entirely filled her with dread. Unwilling to confront her feelings just yet, she sighed before she turned to him. He'd woken up and was studying her. He couldn't read her mind, could he? "We never had dinner. Are you hungry?"

He chuckled. "Always."

Lisa looked at her watch. "How about pizza from Donatello's?"

His eyes lit up. "Do you really think I'd say no?"

She climbed out of bed, wrapped herself in a robe, and padded into the kitchen in search of the take-out menu in the one drawer designated for junk. Donatello's was everyone's favorite pizzeria in Emerald Ridge and, recognizing their strengths, only served pizza.

Twenty different kinds. Her favorite pie was the mushroom and onion. Pulling out the menu and closing the drawer where she kept it, she turned, and the last of her breath escaped from her lungs.

Sander had followed her in, chest bare and clad only in his jeans. He stood beneath the glow of the overhead kitchen chandelier, and the light and shadow emphasized the lines of his body. She took a moment to admire his strong physique and catch her breath. He might spend most of his time designing ranches rather than working them, but his chest, arms, and shoulders were well-defined and clearly those of a man who stayed in shape. The light dusting of hair that she'd so admired earlier was a darker honey color than his dirty-blond locks. He moved with the ease of a man comfortable in his own skin, probably the thing she found most attractive about him.

Her gaze rose to meet him, and his hazel eyes twinkled. His mouth twitched, and a dimple flashed in one cheek. Suddenly, he stood straighter and…was he flexing?

She shook her head as he chuckled quietly. Needing to get ahold of herself and the situation, she thrust the menu toward him. "Favorite toppings?"

He took the menu from her, but didn't look at it. Instead, he kept his attention solely on her. Her skin heated as his gaze started with her eyes, moved down to her breasts and legs and back up to her eyes again. She couldn't decide if she wanted to leap into his arms or hide behind the counter. Instead, she remained frozen in place, trying to remember why they were here.

Finally, he broke the silence. "Sausage, onions, and peppers."

He might as well have said, "You." In fact, by the gleam in his eye, she thought that's what he might be thinking.

Except he handed her back the menu. Whatever else might be going through his mind, he was *talking* about pizza toppings. And she hated sausage. She shuddered. "So either two pies, or a variety of slices."

They settled on a variety of slices, and she called in their order.

The silence in the kitchen stretched, and for the first time since Sander came over, she didn't know what to do. Talk? Go back to bed? Ask what was going through his mind? She wasn't sure she wanted to know.

She'd thought sex with Sander, even though they were just friends, would be no big deal. Except, it was. A *really big deal*, at least for her. And while she had no regrets—none—it did make going back to being just friends harder than she'd thought. If she were brave, she'd pull out a chair and tell him they needed to talk.

But what would happen then? What if she scared him away? She didn't want to scare him away. She might even like having sex with him again—her mouth watered just thinking about that. So, instead of talking, she did what she always did when she had a problem to work out. She baked.

There was time to work on the rugelach while they waited for the pizza to arrive, so she pulled the chilled dough out of the refrigerator and grabbed the ingredients for the filling, mindlessly focusing on what was needed for the cookies rather than her heart. Together, they mixed the filling—cinnamon, sugar, walnuts, raisins, and apricot preserves. Her heartbeat slowed as she got into a rhythm, her breathing evened out.

She sneaked a glance at Sander rolling out the dough, and laughed at his lopsided results.

"Here," she said, "like this." But as she placed her hands over his to show him how to roll out the dough and its yeasty aroma combined with the spicy scent of him, her knees weakened.

"I've got it," he said, his voice low.

Their bodies found myriad ways of touching as they maneuvered around each other, spreading the filling, cutting the dough, and rolling it into the distinctive triangular crescent shape.

"Can I have that spoon?" she asked, reaching across the counter.

Sander nodded and handed it over. Their hands tangled and the spoon fell to the counter with a clatter.

He shook his head and tried again.

"Cut the dough like this, and then add a small amount of filling." Her words came out breathless. Zings of electricity passed along her spine, knocking her off-balance. For the first time, she thanked whoever had designed her kitchen for making it small enough that she and Sander had to touch when they worked together. Even if it made their friendship more confusing.

By the time their pizza was delivered, she wasn't sure if she should throw the rugelach into the fridge and head back to bed, sit down with Sander and have another heart-to-heart conversation, or run away to her mother's house and hide.

Instead, she preheated the oven and reached for plates.

Sander stepped behind her, his body a wall of heat against her back. "Let me get them."

He was taller. It made sense. But her craving for his body warred with her brain, which argued that they were friends. And friends didn't have sex.

Except they had. *Mind-blowing sex*.

So what did that make them? And where did they go from here? Add in her need for independence, her thoughts were muddled like an omelet.

Silence stretched as they pulled their slices onto their plates, grabbed napkins and drinks, and sat at her kitchen table. The table where she'd hoped to have small family dinners. Sander would make a great— She shook her head to get the image out of her head.

He didn't want children.

"What are we doing?" Her question popped out of her mouth on its own, much like her conversation on their date about wanting children, and caught her off guard. Emotions hummed beneath her surface, like a million ants crawling across her skin.

It caught Sander mid-bite. He chewed the pizza in his mouth, his jaw tensing and releasing in time to her own heartbeat, which pattered as she waited for his answer. He put the rest of his slice on his plate and wiped his hands.

"I assume the correct answer isn't eating pizza," he deadpanned, meeting her gaze.

She'd tried to avoid this conversation, but she should have known she'd fail. She'd never been one to run away from anything, no matter how scary, and she wasn't about to start now. Instead, she blurted, "So… are we still friends? Or something more?"

She swallowed, wishing she'd found a more graceful way of asking her question, but it was too late now.

He ran a hand over the top of his head. "I know we said we could be friends, and that you were okay with being friends who have sex." He quirked his mouth up in a half smile. "And just so you're not wondering, what we did back there was wonderful. But being with you has only made me want you more, not less."

Part of her thrilled to hear those words. Another part of her agreed with him—she yearned for him even more than she had before. But a third part of her—the *hated* part—knew that sex wasn't the answer. Sex by itself, without the promises that went along with it, was never the answer. Not for her, at least.

"I feel the same." She couldn't meet his gaze as she spoke, but he reached for her hand.

He squeezed, forcing her to look at him anyway. "So what do we do?"

His question made her throat constrict.

"I don't know," she admitted. "But I don't know how to be friends with someone who makes me feel like this. I thought I could keep things separate, but I don't think I can." Like separating a yolk from the egg white, there was always something that bled into the other.

The light in his eyes dimmed. "I don't want to lose you."

She bit her lip. "I don't want to lose you either. But I don't see how we can avoid hurting each other."

He let his head fall forward. "That's the last thing I'd ever want to do. But we're good together. How can friendship be wrong?"

She wasn't hungry anymore and pushed her plate away. "It's not wrong. But I'm just not sure it's possible. If we weren't both so attracted to each other, it might work. But one or both of us is going to feel pressured to give up on our dreams."

Lisa stared at the two empty chairs at the table. She wanted them filled with kids. She wanted childish laughter and baby cries and a husband who shouldered the responsibility with her. Willingly.

Sander, sprawled in the chair, fit well, in every possible scenario. But his dreams weren't hers.

"I can't be the one to take away your dreams," he ground out.

"And I can't be the one to pressure you into something you don't want."

Her preheated oven beeped, but she ignored it.

"I'm sorry," she said, holding back tears.

"I'm sorry too."

He rose, placed a hand on her shoulder, and walked back into the bedroom. She shut her eyes, trying to swallow the huge lump in her throat. When he returned a moment later, fully dressed, her stomach lurched.

"I think I have to say goodbye," he whispered.

His boots echoed through her house. And when the front door clicked shut, she dropped her head in her hands and wept.

Chapter Six

The next day, after a sleepless night, Sander looked up at the knock on his office door, rubbed his eyes, and ushered Amelia Garland toward the chair on the other side of his desk.

"Hey," he said. "What can I do for you?"

Amelia was his most trusted contractor. Older than him by about ten years, blonde, fit, and whip-smart, she had worked with Sander for years and he trusted her judgment completely. She was carrying a tablet, and when she sat and positioned it on her lap, he saw a copy of the architectural ranch plans he'd been working on.

"I've been pricing out the costs for the ranch at Emerald Creek, and I think we have a problem." She pulled up a spreadsheet and turned the tablet toward Sander.

His eyes widened. "Holy cow. Since when is lumber that expensive?" He did a double take, in case his lack of sleep jumbled the numbers.

It hadn't.

"Thanks to the strain on the power grid after the last set of major storms, the supply chain has suffered in a lot of unexpected ways. Not to mention the cost of fuel and a few wildfires in areas that usually provide our choicest maple. Before I go back to the client, do you want to make any suggestions for substitutions?"

Sander shut his eyes, his mind spinning. He tried to focus on what Amelia was saying, but he still couldn't get Lisa and the incredible sex they'd had last night out of his mind. "Yes, but I'm gonna need a little time to readjust things. Email me what you've got and I'll do my best. In the meantime, see if you can head off the client before they get on our tail about what's taking so long."

Amelia nodded before rising. "We can always blame it on the holidays. You know how things slow down at this time of year."

Blaming others for his problems wasn't Sander's style. "I guess, but I hate to be that kind of architect. When I set a timeline, I like to stick to it."

She nodded. "Got any big plans? I'll bet it'll be fun with Kelsey, Trevor, and the triplets."

Sander smiled, remembering how much fun she'd been at that age and grew wistful. But multiplied by three? He huffed.

"I'm not sure what I'm doing, actually. With the kids busy with their families for the most part, I might just use the time to catch up on some of my work." Anything to keep his attention off Lisa, although he suspected nothing would get the incredible woman out of his mind. He tilted his chin toward her tablet. "Especially now that my to-do list just got longer."

Amelia frowned. "You can't skip the holidays," she said and paused. "You know you're always welcome to celebrate with us."

"Thank you. That's kind of you. But I'll be okay. Besides, if I chose to celebrate Christmas with someone else's family other than my own, I might have to face down a mutiny."

She laughed and held up her hands. "God forbid I get in the middle of a Fortune mutiny." With a wave, she left.

Silence descended. Usually, he relished disappearing into the lines and planes and angles. Creating someone's dream ranch satisfied him in ways nothing else could. The focus and vision he needed exercised a part of his brain, and gratified a piece of his soul.

Usually.

Today, those lines, planes, and angles didn't sing. They didn't give him a rush of excitement. They were just geometric pieces of a puzzle that was supposed to be three-dimensional but was coming in flat. With a sigh, he rose from his desk and walked outside, letting the cool breeze clear his head.

Sex with Lisa…he hated calling it "sex" because it had been so much more than that. They'd come together as one. His soul had connected with hers. His entire body froze. *His soul?* He'd never felt anything like what he felt last night with Lisa. God, had it only been last night? Time had stopped, restarted, and surrounded him, so he no longer knew where one day ended and the next began. All he knew was he'd had Lisa for a brief time…and lost her. He shut his eyes as desolation swamped him.

Spinning around, he walked back inside and scanned his desk with disdain. Moments flashed in his head, like a reel on his social media, and he gulped. Lisa hugging her nieces but smiling at him. Or looking at him sympathetically as he told her about Linc and Finn. Or lying beneath him, their bodies entwined. Until he and Lisa had realized they couldn't be together.

His throat closed, and he swallowed. Goddammit. One woman, one singular—albeit beautiful, intelligent, and funny—woman, could make him lose all interest in other things. How was that possible? He should not be this off-kilter.

Somehow, he needed to get back his equilibrium, find his joy again. And this time, without Lisa. They were compatible in every way except what they wanted for their futures. And that one obstacle was too big to overcome. Because no matter how much he desired his own happiness, he wasn't about to sacrifice someone else's dream.

The man he planned to be was independent, work-driven, and responsible. And that meant sitting down to work even if he wasn't inspired. With renewed determination, he sat behind his desk once again, pulled up the plans for the ranch, and tried to focus on ways to sub out materials with lower cost options. An hour later, he pushed his tablet away, rubbed his eyes, and rolled his shoulders. He was a lucky bastard. Thanks to the luck of the birth-draw, he was a Fortune. He'd never have to worry about money. He could attain any dream he wanted. Unlike his client, who'd asked him to stick to the budget.

Unlike Lisa, who couldn't afford IVF.

He groaned. Why did everything remind him of her?

He needed a better distraction. Grabbing his phone from his pocket, he dialed his friend Stuart. "Want to grab a beer?"

At Stu's affirmation, he pocketed his phone, set his hat squarely on his head, reached for his keys, and left. Ten minutes later, he pulled up to the Cowpoke Brewery. Situated on a side street on the edge of Emerald Ridge and boasting the best beer in the region, the brewery was Sander's favorite spot to unwind. The noisy bar was just the place for him to get a break from his thoughts.

He sat at his favorite table in the back, facing the door and ordered two Jester Kings. The wooden table had countless initials and names carved into it from years' worth of loyal patrons. Not only were the seats wide and comfortable, they were conducive to lengthy stays for drinking beer and hanging with friends. The waitstaff knew just when to approach and when to leave you alone. Glancing around, he noted that the bar's only nod to the holidays was greenery around the window, bells around the doorway, and a few sprigs of mistletoe hanging above the mahogany bar. Almost daring someone to steal a drunken kiss. Sander knew there were probably more decorations in the event space in the back, where the owners hosted activities for the tourists. But he was comfortable right here.

Stu walked in and headed straight for Sander. Pals since grade school, Stu was the one he confided in when life got tough. Stu mined Sander for financial and ranch advice. And together, they commiserated on their lousy luck with women.

"You look like shit," Stu said. He nodded to the waiter, who brought the drinks Sander had ordered, and took a big gulp, wiping the froth off his lip with the back of his hand.

"Nice," Sander said.

"Am I wrong?"

"How the heck should I know?" Sander grimaced. "I don't spend all my time staring at myself in the mirror."

"That explains a lot," his friend said with a wink. The two of them each took a sip in silence. Then Stu asked, "Have you read the lumber futures reports? The prices are *wild*."

"Tell me about it. I'm in the middle of redoing plans for a client, because if we turn them in based on these numbers, they're gonna throw a fit."

Stu pinned him with a stare that made Sander squirm. "So is the price of lumber causing your crappy mood this afternoon, or is it something else?"

"It's certainly not helping, but it's more than that."

Stu leaned back and stretched his arm out across the back of the chair. He waited his friend out.

Sander scowled before launching into what happened between him and Lisa.

"I swear, if it weren't for her need to have a baby, she'd be perfect."

"You know perfect doesn't exist," Stu said.

"That's because you haven't met Lisa."

Stu recoiled. "Are you saying what I think you're saying?"

"No, scratch that. She's not perfect. Neither am I. But if I were to write up a list of everything I'd want in a partner, she'd check off every single box."

"Darn, that stinks," Stu said. "I mean, you find the woman of your dreams, and can't have her? I'm sorry, that's rough."

"Now you see why I'm like this," Sander grumbled.

"I do. I wish I had advice for you." He brightened. "Maybe the holidays will distract you. What are the Fortune plans?"

The way he said "Fortune" showed he figured there was some grand family plan. And there usually was. But this year, Sander wasn't in the mood.

He shrugged. "We'll do our typical Christmas Eve dinner at my house, but then everyone has their own plans with their families," he said. "And I'm really not in the ho-ho-ho mood. Even if the family is coming over tonight to help me decorate."

Still, despite the drag on his festive spirits, he couldn't help reminiscing about holidays gone by… The huge Christmas tree his dad and uncles would drag into the house; how his mother would oversee the exact placement of all the ornaments, especially the handmade ones; the gifts wrapped under the tree and the anticipation that built to a fever pitch. His brother had tried to keep it up after he and Marlene got married, with a few changes to accommodate his wife's needs. Once Sander had to take over the festivities, he'd done his best to make sure his nieces and nephews and Linc and Kelsey enjoyed the holiday as much as he had. He'd tried to make memories for them too. And based on how much they all looked forward to it and wanted to celebrate with their families, he was pretty sure he'd achieved his goal. That knowledge should have made him feel proud. But he was just so damned tired.

Stu shook his head. "I'm not going to force you, but I'd hate for you to regret not celebrating. So if you change your mind, even last minute, know that you're always welcome to have Christmas dinner with us."

He raised his drink in a toast. "Thanks."

After Stu finished his drink and left, Sander remained, nursing the last of his beer and thinking about regrets. Maybe it was the time of year. Maybe he'd woken up on the wrong side of the bed. Whatever the reason, the weight of regret squeezed him tight, like the octopus story he used to read Kelsey at bedtime. A small smile escaped him. If the road to hell was paved with good intentions, its sidewalks were filled with regrets. And he'd be damned if he was going to make anyone else suffer because of him.

Chapter Seven

That evening, Sander's front door burst open with shouts of, "Santa's elves have arrived!"

Roth and Jax dragged in a huge tree. Almost immediately, the house filled with the scent of pine. Priscilla and Zara carried platters of food, adding an overtone of garlic and spices. Sander inhaled deeply. Antonia, with the help of Sofia's two kids, Kaitlin and Jackson, took the babies—her one-year-old daughter, Georgie, Jax's baby Liam, and Trevor's triplets—into the playroom to keep them occupied and out of the way. Their babbles and coos added to the din, but softened it somehow. Or maybe they just softened his heart.

"Make sure to save us some food, please," Antonia yelled as she maneuvered strollers and baby carriers.

Roth grabbed one of her hands and pulled her back toward him for a moment. "Will do." He kissed his fiancée's cheek and went to help the others.

Sander watched them wistfully as they disappeared down the hall.

Wistfully? He shook his head. He really was off his game today.

Despite his scroogy outlook, he'd brought the tree

stand down from the attic, so he directed Roth and Jax to the living room. He'd cleaned out the corner as he always did during Christmas to make way for the tree. Once it was secured in its spot, they left the room, returning a little while later with boxes of ornaments.

Laughter from the kitchen drew him there.

"What's all this?"

The counter was covered with pizza, salads, and drinks.

Antonia looked at him askance. "You can't possibly think we'd do anything without food, can you? Do you even *know* us anymore?"

Sander laughed and his mood lightened. "Very true."

"Armies have risen and fallen due to a lack of provisions," she said with a wink.

"We wouldn't want that," he retorted, grabbing a slice of pepperoni pizza.

Pizza. He and Lisa had ordered pizza together, but they had never had a chance to eat it. He stared at his slice for a moment, lost in what might have been. Chatter from the living room drew him back.

Kelsey and Priscilla unwrapped ornaments, reminiscing about memories each one evoked.

"Oh, look at this one," Priscilla said softly. "Linc made it."

About the size of a grapefruit, the flat clay was painted red with a child's handprint pressed into it.

"Remember how we were all making these, and he kept protesting, but did it anyway?"

Kelsey nodded. "And his smile afterward was bigger than all of ours combined."

Sander's chest constricted as he watched his niece place the handprint on the tree, wipe away a tear, and continue unwrapping the other ornaments.

"Aw, Kels, look at this one!" Priscilla called.

Three Styrofoam balls, attached at crazy angles, dangled from a string, with toothpick arms and a black felt hat. Sparkly stars were pasted all over it.

"That has to be the world's most crooked snowman ever," she said, shaking her head. "I don't know why you haven't thrown that away."

Sander leaned over and kissed the top of his daughter's head. "Because you made it."

"Yeah, when I was *five*!"

"Then its odd shape is forgivable," he answered. "On the tree it goes." Despite his lack of Christmas spirit, even he got caught up in everyone's excitement, and he found a branch next to Linc's ornament for the crooked snowman.

As they each told stories or complained about the homemade ornaments, Sander thought back fondly to when the kids were little. So much chaos and unpredictability. At the time, he hadn't been able to appreciate anything, so overwhelmed was he by responsibility. Now, though, well, his memories were rosy-hued with time, and a part of him wished he could go back to those days, just for a few minutes. They'd all been together, a united group that faced the world as one. Today, they were all more independent, more solitary.

At least, that's how it felt to Sander.

Kelsey approached and wrapped her arm around

him. "Are you sure you won't join us for Christmas Day, Dad?"

"We'll have Christmas Eve dinner here, as usual," he said. "I have gifts for the triplets and don't want to miss out on their reactions. But I'm gonna let you five have your holiday on your own."

"It won't be the same without you."

He laughed. "You'll be so busy with three little ones you won't even know I'm gone, sweet girl. I promise you'll be sick of me by the time we're finished with Christmas Eve dinner."

Everyone disagreed, although Zara shot him a look of understanding, but Sander stood his ground. Even if he was inclined to spend the day with his family, he didn't want his mood to interfere with their enjoyment of the holiday.

Sander looked fondly once again at his daughter. "I remember you when you were the triplets' ages. Tearing through the wrapping paper, putting box tops on your head. If you could have figured out a way to climb up the Christmas tree, you would have."

"Now multiply that by three," Kelsey said.

His jaw dropped in mock horror. "Good luck, you're going to need it."

"Dad!"

"You know I'm pulling your leg. I can't wait to see the three of them crawl through the chaos." *And then escape for some peace and quiet afterward.*

"You're sure you won't be lonely?" Her worried gaze tore at his heart.

He grasped her shoulders and looked her squarely

in her green eyes. "I won't be lonely." He pulled her into a hug.

Liar, his brain screamed. He coughed in an attempt to hide his roiling thoughts, backing away before Kelsey could sense something was amiss.

"All right. But I'm making your favorite Christmas cookies, so you'd better plan to save extras for Christmas Day."

"As if my grandbabies aren't enough of an enticement." His stomach rumbled. "I always have room for cookies. Lots of chocolate crinkles, right?"

She laughed.

Trevor and Zara unpacked the garland and wound it around the tree, filling in empty spots, while Roth added red and silver balls.

"Uncle Sander, where's the box with the stockings?" Roth asked.

He frowned. "It should be with all the other Christmas boxes."

"I'll go look again," he said. A few minutes later, he returned, box in hand and a sheepish look on his face. "It was in the back."

No matter how successful his kids became as adults, bring them into this house, the one they grew up in, and they reverted to the blind children who couldn't find a sock right in front of their faces.

Sander opened the box and pulled out the stockings. "Do you guys want to take them home with you?"

His kids looked at each other, then as one, shook their heads. "No, leave them here. Hanging where they always have."

For some reason, a lump formed in his throat, and he swallowed as he stuck the hooks on the mantel. Kelsey, Roth, Harris, Priscilla, and Zara. The last stocking he pulled was Linc's. Sorrow made his heart ache.

Zara took the stocking from him and hung it up with the rest of them. "Nothing has to change, even if everything already has."

He leaned down to his niece and she blushed.

"You doing okay, sweetheart?" he asked.

Zara shrugged and forced a smile. "It's Christmastime. Magic and love and presents. Who wouldn't be okay?"

He knew better than to be fooled by her words, even if he hadn't heard the despair in her voice.

He pulled her aside. "I was at the Equestrian Estate earlier."

She swallowed.

"Ran into Finn," he added. "The guy looks torn up." For a lot of reasons, but he suspected one of the biggest ones was his niece.

Zara gazed out the window, blinking furiously. He hated to pry, but she'd always been the quiet one.

"How do you feel about him being back in town?"

She shrugged. "He's free to be wherever he wants."

"That's not what I asked, Z."

Spinning around, her eyes flashed, before she banked the pain that bled from them. "I can't discuss this here…now. Please."

Her voice broke on the "please" and her pain tore at him.

"Okay," he whispered.

She walked away and he blinked, staring at the various stockings in a row. Each one reflected the kids' varied personalities as children. Each one helped make Christmas a family affair. As he stared at the kids putting the finishing touches on the decorations, at the stockings on the mantel, he wondered what the future held for any of them.

When Sander had walked out of Lisa's house, she'd crumbled to the ground. Now, a day later, her body physically ached with despair. She hadn't been this devastated since finding out she couldn't afford IVF. She'd gone back to bed. But the sheets smelled like him—like *them*—and she'd ripped them off the bed and threw them into the washing machine with half a bottle of bleach. Tears of sadness and anger fought to escape, and each time she swallowed, the lump in her throat expanded. She'd remade the bed, but those sheets scratched her skin, reminding her of other things that had recently scratched her, namely, Sander's whiskers. So she'd put on her softest pajamas, which happened to also be her warmest, and she'd lain in bed, sweating and awake.

When her sister called to suggest a trip to the store together, her broken heart urged her to say no. But her mouth had said yes, and she'd somehow dragged herself into the shower. And now she was clean and ready to go.

Maybe shopping would get her out of her funk and into the holiday spirit.

A short time later, she and Sara were walking

through the gift shop, searching the holiday merchandise for anything Hanukkah related. She'd already decorated her classroom in blue, white, silver, red, gold, and green for the winter holidays. The variety of colors reminded her of a bottle of multicolored sprinkles. And she had her menorah and candles all ready to go at home. But she loved the holidays and always looked for ways to freshen up her celebrations.

At least, she had in the past. Today, she was going through the motions, hoping muscle memory would push her through and remind her of the joy she couldn't for the life of her find right now.

"What about this?" Her sister held up a string of snowflakes with tiny white lights attached to them. "It's not Hanukkah, but the winter theme is pretty."

Lisa smiled, despite herself. "Mmm, it is. That would look nice in my classroom." She glanced toward the front of the store. "Although the likelihood of snow here in Emerald Ridge is about as likely as Santa coming down my chimney." She placed two boxes of the lights in her cart and continued down the holiday aisle.

"Did I tell you David and I are going skiing in Colorado?"

Lisa's heart lurched. She and Jordan had loved skiing in Aspen when they were first married. Or rather, *he'd* loved it. Lisa was more of an après-ski person, but even she had enjoyed a little time on the slopes with her husband. "Aspen?"

Her sister's expression turned wary. "Yeah. You okay with that?"

She tested the memory and found it didn't hurt as

much as it used to. "I don't own the town, Sara. Of course I am. Kids going with you or staying with Mom and Dad?"

"Staying with them. Our folks are dying to spoil them."

"Me too. Maybe I'll steal them for a day or so." She continued strolling down the aisle, trying to distract herself with ideas of what she could do with her nieces. "It'll be good for the two of you to get away together."

Sara smiled, a wistful look on her face. "We haven't gone away, just the two of us, since before the kids were born."

Lisa looked at her sideways. "And you want to spend your time *skiing*?"

"What's wrong with skiing?"

"Absolutely nothing," Lisa said. "But I can think of plenty of other activities that would burn just as many calories, without making you cold."

Her sister burst out laughing. "Trust me, so can I."

"Good. Just checking."

"Speaking of sex…" Sara began.

"Wait, I thought we were talking about skiing."

Her sister smacked Lisa's arm. "What's going on with you and Sander?"

Oof, what a segue. A knot of disappointment formed in the pit of her stomach. "Nothing, unfortunately."

Sara paused, turning to face Lisa. "Wait, I thought you were into him."

"I am. I mean, I was. But he's dead set against kids, and I'm, well, not." Her chin trembled, but she was not going to burst into tears in the middle of the store.

Her sister's eyes filled with sympathy. "I'm so sorry." She gave her a hug.

Lisa breathed in the familiar scent of Sara's hair and tried to calm down, carried back to their childhood when they snuggled under the blanket together, giggling and whispering when they were supposed to be sleeping. But the hug of sympathy made her want to cry even more, so she pulled away.

"I don't suppose there's any possibility of changing his mind?"

Her chest ached. *If only.* "I couldn't live with myself if I did that, if it's even doable. He's raised his daughter, nieces and nephews, putting aside his own needs for theirs. How can I possibly push him to once again put aside his dreams for me? And what kind of person would I be if I tried?"

"Yeah, forcing kids on someone who doesn't want them won't work," Sara agreed. "It's too bad though. It sounds like the two of you were good together."

"I thought we could be." Her shoulders sagged. "Honestly, as much as I wish things could work out between us, my focus needs to be on starting a family. It's what I've wanted forever, and I don't want to wait any longer." She straightened her shoulders, trying to force her body to accept the goal her heart had settled on. Even if part of that heart ached for Sander.

Her sister smiled. "I remember how we'd play house together and you always had six baby dolls that you'd drag around with you."

Lisa gave a half smile. "Oh gosh, and half of them I dragged by the hair."

"I wasn't going to say anything...but hopefully you've gotten past that little habit." She nudged Lisa, who nudged her right back. "Seriously, you're an amazing teacher and aunt," Sara continued. "You'll be a fantastic mother. And if you want to go ahead with adoption, I think you should. There are a ton of kids out there waiting for good homes."

Lisa headed toward the checkout area, her mind spinning. "You know, I've always pictured myself with a baby." Of course, that picture had included a husband. An image of Sander flashed in her mind and she shook her head to clear it. "But if I'm going to adopt, I have even more options."

As they unloaded their carts, her sister glanced at her. "Would you consider adopting an older child?"

"I'm not really sure," Lisa said. "This is the first time I'm really thinking about it. But I love teaching middle school. Honestly, I love kids. *Period.* I don't really care how old they are. And while I'd like to adopt a baby and have the experience of being their mother for almost their entire life, I don't think I'd say no if there was an older child in need of a mom."

Her eyes filled with tears as she considered the implication of her words. She'd been focused for years on having a baby. But now that she was open to adoption, the possibilities seemed endless. Her pulse raced as doubts filled her. What if she wasn't qualified? What if they turned her down?

"I think I need to go talk to someone in social services or to someone who used to work for the Texas Royale Private Adoption Agency. If only to find out what the process is and whether I'm even qualified as a single mom."

"Do you want company?"

She hugged her sister. "I love that you're willing, but I have to do this on my own. At least to start." When she'd imagined being a mom, it had always included a husband by her side. Since that part of the dream was looking less and less likely, she needed to embrace her independence, to start out as she meant to continue. And that meant going it alone.

They walked outside with their purchases. "Okay, but I'm here and willing if you need anything."

Her family was always supportive of her. She'd never have gotten over Jordan's death without them. When she'd fallen apart, her parents and her sister were the ones who had sewn her back together. She owed them everything.

Turning to her sister, she enfolded her in a fierce hug. "I love you, Sara."

Her sister hugged her back. "You're not so bad, yourself."

"I'm serious," Lisa said. "I couldn't do any of this without you."

Her sister took a step back, brushed a curl off Lisa's forehead, and nodded. "I love you too. But you don't give yourself enough credit. You're the most determined, loving, and capable person I know. If anyone can do this, you can. Don't ever doubt it."

Spinning around, Sara got into her car, waved, and drove away.

Smiling through her tears, Lisa followed her out of

the parking lot, vowing to see her dream through. And to somehow, figure out a way to live without Sander.

Sander climbed out of his truck and walked across the wide expanse of property to his daughter's ranch. Kelsey stood, hip cocked, talking to her contractor and pointing to her forewoman's house. He paused before approaching, letting his pride envelop him. His daughter was smart and strong, and while he would have enjoyed helping her with the Fortune 8 ranch, he admired her determination to do it on her own. It was up and running, and as far as he could tell, working beautifully.

Still standing off to the side, he studied the body language of the contractor and his assistants. He knew their reputation was excellent, but after what she'd been through with her former employees, he'd worried they wouldn't take someone so young—and female—seriously. But nothing in their posture or expressions indicated anything other than compliance. Maybe it was the fact that she'd gotten the ranch up and running in record time. Or maybe his daughter exuded confidence when she dealt with them. Whatever the reason, he exhaled with relief. When the contractor moved back toward the forewoman's house, Sander approached his daughter.

"Spying on me?" She smiled, reassuring him her nose wasn't out of joint.

"More like on *them*," he said, nodding his head toward the workers. "I knew you'd have everything under control."

Her cheeks reddened. "Thanks, Dad."

Sander cleared his throat. "I do have one question though."

She waited him out, and he smiled to himself. His baby girl had learned her tactics from him. Silence could be used to one's advantage.

"Are your lumber price estimates as high as ours have been?"

Her eyes widened. "It's crazy, right? Tom is doing what he can to offset it, but the numbers are wild. What are you doing?"

"The same thing. I've got a client who is going to go crazy if I give her the real cost. So we're trying to substitute and find other sources. I was just wondering if you were having any luck."

She turned toward the truck. "Tom! Got a sec?"

The man lumbered over, nodded to Sander. "Sure, what's up."

Sander and Tom discussed the lumber prices, brainstorming solutions and sharing sources. When the contractor left, Sander turned back to Kelsey. "I like his suggestions." He made some notes in his phone, planning to pass along the information to Amelia.

"You didn't really think I'd work with someone you couldn't depend on, did you?"

"Nope, not if you're my daughter."

Her grin, as usual, blew him away.

He stuffed his hands in his pockets. "You know, you were right about yesterday."

She arched a brow. "Care to elaborate?"

"About decorating for Christmas. It was nice to have everyone together under the same roof."

She nodded. "See, I do know things."

He hugged her. "You know how proud I am of you, right? The way you balance work and the babies. You've taken to them so naturally. I'm…kind of in awe. All of you act like having kids is the most natural thing in the world. You're so much calmer than I was back then."

"You did what you had to do in a lousy situation, Dad. And you gave us safety and security and love. You made us who we are today."

His eyes misted, and he pulled her into another hug to hide his reaction.

"If anyone deserves a break, Dad, it's you. So if you don't want all the Christmas crazy, we understand and we're not going to begrudge you peace and quiet…or time alone with anyone who might catch your fancy."

She grinned at him and he shook his head.

"That's enough out of you, Kels, but I appreciate it."

After saying goodbye to her, he returned to his truck to head back to his office.

As it so often did, Lisa's face popped into his mind, and he shook his head. One of these days, he'd stop thinking about her. They hadn't known each other long. Clearly, he'd forget about her soon. In the meantime, he'd have to learn to push past the ache in his chest every time he thought of her, to stop wanting to share his pride in his daughter with her, not to crave her challah every time his stomach growled. Today, however, wasn't such a day.

Today his mind was filled with questions about her. After all the Christmas decorations were hung, he'd wanted to find out about her holiday celebrations. Did she decorate? Spend Hanukkah with her family? Enjoy picking out just the right gifts for each person on her list? Heck, did she even have a list? If things had been different, how would they handle the two different holidays? His mind leaped to fill in the blanks—they'd have a huge shindig with his family before retiring to his home to celebrate just the two of them. Although, if he knew Lisa, she'd probably want to spend most of her time with all the babies. He smiled, picturing Lisa's delight over sharing the festivities with the triplets. She'd probably be down on the floor with them, helping them open their gifts. His heart squeezed. What did she do for Hanukkah? He'd have to ask her the next time he saw her.

If he saw her.

He snorted. Their paths hadn't crossed under ordinary circumstances. What made him think they would now that he knew her? But he couldn't stop wondering what her holiday was like, which was kind of weird given his lack of Christmas spirit this year. He'd read that Hanukkah lasted eight days. That was the extent of his knowledge. Disappointment flared. He'd lost out on knowing more, on experiencing her holiday. If they'd stayed together...heck, if they'd let their relationship develop into something, he'd have gotten the chance to celebrate with her. And somehow, he just knew he'd missed something special.

His heart quickened, making him pause. Why did

the thought of celebrating with her bring him more interest than the thought of doing so with his own family? That couldn't be right. He loved his daughter, loved his nieces and nephews as if they were his children. Their own kids brought a smile to his face every time he saw them. He could only imagine how much fun all of them would be at Christmas. So why wasn't he excited about celebrating the holidays with them?

He tried to figure it out as he drove back home. He loved and admired each of his "kids." Only Zara still worried him, and that was because he loved her so much. And Kelsey? Well, nothing could keep him away from his daughter.

So it wasn't *them* he wanted to avoid.

Was it Christmas? He scoffed as he removed his boots and walked through the cavernous and thankfully empty house toward his office. His house smelled of cinnamon and leather, and everywhere he looked, he couldn't help but see evidence of the upcoming holiday.

He pictured all the kids, tumbling over each other to unwrap gifts, rushing around in their pj's and waking every adult up at god-awful-early in the morning. He couldn't wait to see them all in their holiday excitement.

But he wanted time to himself. Time to breathe. He wanted to enjoy his family and then retreat to the quiet of his own home. Was that wrong of him? It shouldn't be. But then why did the guilt eat at him? Kelsey was fine with his plan. He swore under his breath. He hadn't actually spoken to his nieces and nephews specifically about it, but when his daughter had asked him about Christmas Day, they'd all been there and nodded along.

He pulled out his phone and dialed Roth.

"Stupid question," he said, when his nephew picked up. "Are you okay with me skipping Christmas Day?"

"Sure," Roth said. "We talked about it the other day."

"No, I talked about it. You and your siblings just nodded along. I don't want to upset anyone by not participating."

"Uncle Sander, do you really think we'd keep our opinions to ourselves? Have you ever known us to do that?"

Sander laughed. "Not that I can remember." Roth was always the practical one. It was one of the reasons he was so successful.

"I guarantee no one is taking it personally."

"With all your new family and job responsibilities, whether or not I spend the holidays with you all is probably not even on your radar," Sander agreed.

"We've always got time for you," Roth protested.

"No, I get it. And for the record, I'm damned proud of you. Of all of you. You've grown to be independent and I couldn't be happier."

"You're still the glue that holds us together," Roth said, "even if we have lives of our own now. Maybe it's time for you to find someone for yourself."

Sander paused. "Thank you. It means a lot, especially coming from you."

He hung up the phone and scoffed.

Could he actually have empty-nest syndrome? Everyone he knew was in the throes of family life. But he'd focused on family life early, when all his friends were out partying and enjoying the freedom of their twenties. It had taken a while for his family to move into homes of their own. Kelsey was still in the throes of moving—she still had a few boxes left at his house—and Harris, who typically traveled between Dallas and Emerald Ridge, had finally settled down with Sofia and her kids. Everyone else, though, was settled on their own. Now that he was ready to focus on himself, all of them were busy. And where he usually could fall back on his family...well, they were busy with their own lives. He shook his head. His life schedule had never coincided with those around him. Silly of him to think it would now.

He rammed his hat back on his head. Stupid emotions. Wallowing in loss wasn't going to change anything. In fact, it would waste this precious freedom that he actually had. All his friends were probably jealous of his ability to do what he wanted when he wanted. And Lisa? It was a pity they couldn't be together, but there were other women out there for him. Roth was right. There had to be someone for him, and maybe it was time for him to look for her. A woman whose dreams more closely aligned with his. Wallowing wasn't going to help him find them either.

Coffee. That's what he needed. Caffeine solved everything. He turned around and headed into the center of town.

Chapter Eight

Lisa took a step back and surveyed her living room, warmth and joy flowing through her. Although Hanukkah wasn't a big holiday, especially compared to Christmas, she loved decorating her home with meaningful pieces from her childhood. Each item brought back memories of the love of her family and reminded her of the special times they'd shared.

On the mantel above the fireplace sat three menorahs she'd made in Hebrew school. When she was growing up, her mom had insisted on displaying and using them, much to her embarrassment. Now, though, the crooked candleholders made her smile. Through the archway in the dining room, a large bowl of dreidels sat in the middle of the table on a blue and white table runner, reminding her of the times her grandmother had always insisted on playing dreidel with her and her sister, every time she'd visited.

In the front window sat her large electric menorah, ready for lighting on the first night. Whenever she and her sister had driven through their childhood neighborhood, they'd loved pointing out the houses with the lit menorahs in the windows, identifying with the community they shared even if they didn't know the specific neighbor. And in her kitchen, her favorite menorah, the one she'd bought on her Italian honeymoon with Jordan, sat waiting for candles. She remembered them wandering into a little shop in the Jewish quarter in Rome and trying to decide which menorah to buy. In the end, the shopkeeper had gifted them this one when he heard they were newly married. She exhaled. So many good memories. Maybe that's why she loved the holiday. Checking off her to-do list, she nodded. The menorah and candles were ready. Now she needed the food.

Baking was her salvation. And any holiday that celebrated fried food—after all, the story of Hanukkah glorified oil—was perfect in her book. She sank into her overstuffed chair beneath the window and flipped through her holiday cookbooks. She had several. Donuts were a must. Her nieces loved her sugary jelly ones, and their adorable faces framed with powdered sugar and sticky with jelly were precious. Homemade chocolate gelt, check. And potato pancakes. She'd have to pick a day that wasn't too cold to make them so she could air out her kitchen from all the oil.

Her phone rang, and she marked the pages to save them before answering.

"Is this Lisa Bergen?" a female voice asked.

"Yes." She didn't recognize the voice or the number. *I should have let this go to voicemail.*

"This is Claire from Wee Ones Adoption Agency."

Lisa straightened her spine. Her heart did a flip-flop.

"I'd like to set up an appointment to discuss your adoption application."

She opened her mouth, but no sound came out. *Oh my God, they're calling me!* She tried again, clearing her throat.

"Um, yes, I'd love to. When were you thinking?" *Where's my calendar? Where?* It was on her phone that was currently against her ear. She shook her head and tried to calm herself. But fear and excitement battled in her chest, making everything harder.

"Your application says you're a teacher. How about over the holiday break, say, Tuesday?"

Lisa's fingers shook as she hit Speaker and scrolled to her calendar. It was as if her hands were encased in huge mitts, because no matter what she tapped, it was the wrong app, the wrong month, or the wrong day. Not that it mattered what she'd scheduled that day. She'd cancel. Finally, she reached the right spot on her calendar. She heaved a sigh of relief. The day was free.

"That's perfect. What time?"

"Ten a.m.?"

Lisa nodded and tried to type in the meeting, but again, her trembling fingers kept missing the correct keys.

"I'll see you then."

As soon as the call disconnected, she jumped up and began pacing the room. Her gaze darted from corner to corner, wondering what she should do. Babyproof? Clean? Bake? Oh my gosh, holiday gifts! But as soon as those thoughts entered her head, her rational side gave her a poke.

It's only an interview. You're not leaving with a baby.

Her heart thudded and her breathing slowed. An interview. Just an interview. To see if she were fit to start the process. From everything she'd heard, the process was long and arduous. Her skin turned icy. What if she'd said the wrong thing during the phone call? Or hadn't expressed enough enthusiasm? Or entered it in her calendar wrong and showed up late?

She grabbed her phone, smacked the screen, and scrolled for the calendar. *Tuesday at ten, during her holiday break.* Taking another in a series of deep breaths, she tried to calm down for real this time. This was the first step in a long process. And no one was judged on that initial phone call.

Hands shaking, she dialed her best friend.

"Mel, it's me." Her voice cracked. "I've got an interview with an adoption agency."

Her friend's gasp released the tears Lisa had tried so hard to hold back. "Oh my gosh, I'm so happy for you! That's wonderful."

"I know, right? I'm so scared though."

"Why?" Melissa asked.

"What if I screw everything up?"

Melissa's laugh echoed through the phone. "Oh, please, you're the least likely of anyone anywhere to screw up anything." She lowered her voice. "You were born for this."

Walking over to the mirror hanging next to her front door, Lisa stared hard at her reflection. Her long dark curly hair framed a face tinged with pink and her amber eyes shone with excitement. She'd bitten her lip hard enough to redden it. But Lisa knew what she looked like on the outside. It was the inside that mattered.

"You're right," she said, her confidence returning. "I was."

"You're going to crush the interview, Lis, trust me."

Straightening her shoulders, Lisa murmured out loud, "I'm a teacher. A good human. And I want a baby. I can do this."

"You totally can," Melissa said. "And I want to hear all about it afterward, okay?"

Promising to call her as soon as she'd completed the interview, Lisa hung up.

Her mouth was dry from nerves, so she went into the kitchen to find something to drink. The cool liquid refreshed her, but what she really wanted was coffee and a scone from Emerald Ridge Café. She glanced around, a small smile stretching her mouth. The adoption agency had received her application and called her for an appointment. Right there, that was cause to celebrate.

Grabbing her purse and keys from the counter, she decided to treat herself.

A short drive later, she pulled into a spot directly across the street from the Emerald Ridge Café. The inviting aroma of coffee beans, cinnamon, and cloves emanating from the café made her mouth water. A chalkboard sign outside listed their December special drinks—peppermint lattes, jelly donut coffee, and cinnamon frappé.

After placing her order at the counter, she sat in the corner at one of the tables making mindless circles with her fingers on the blue-checkered tablecloth and tapping her foot to the catchy holiday music coming over the speakers. She loved listening to all the Christmas music playing at this time of year. The festive tunes automatically cheered her up. Even now, her excitement reached a fever pitch. She tapped her foot in time to the music. An overwhelming desire to share her news with her mom and sister filled her. She reached for her phone, but paused, hand hovering over the screen. A busy coffee shop wasn't the place for a conversation, and her news wasn't the kind of thing she should text. They'd want way more details than her fingers could manage.

The bell over the door jingled, drawing her gaze.

Sander.

Her breath caught in her throat. All activity around her faded into the background as she drank in his presence. His arrival shouldn't have surprised her. The Emerald Ridge Café was popular, and they lived in the same town. They were bound to run into each other at some point. But did it have to be right now, when she was so focused on the very thing that prevented them from being together?

He hadn't noticed her yet, and despite how much it hurt, she took advantage of the moment to study him. Still as handsome as ever with his dirty blond hair that curled against his collar, his jeans that showed off his long muscular legs, and his solid forearms, shown off by his sleeves rolled to his elbows. Her pulse leaped. Yet something was off. The set of his shoulders, usually so straight and proud, drooped just a little. Barely noticeable to most, probably, but he reminded her of a plant needing watering. His step was a little less brisk than normal as well. Stuffing his hands in his pockets, he looked at the menu above the counter, a melancholy air around him. People surrounded him, but he was alone.

That was it. He looked lonely.

Her heart squeezed with sympathy. She understood lonely. She *was* lonely, even as hard as she tried to fight it.

When he turned around, order in hand, she raised her arm and waved.

Oh, Lisa, what have you done?

His face brightened, and somewhere deep down, his joy at seeing her warmed her, making all her reservations flee.

"Hey," he said, removing his hat as he approached her table.

"Hey."

They looked at each other in silence for a few beats, before Lisa added, "Would you like to join me?"

He pinned her with his stare, as if plumbing the depths of her being, trying to decipher the hidden meaning behind her words.

"Are you sure?"

Was she? Spending time together was just going to make her miss him more. Then again, maybe it would get easier with frequency. Regardless, a part of her empathized with his obvious suffering. She nodded. They'd run into each other occasionally, and she didn't want to be the kind of person who gave the cold shoulder.

At least, that's what she told herself.

He folded his body onto the chair, placed his hot coffee on the table in front of him, and rested his hat on his lap. Those familiar movements made her ache.

"How have you been?" His deep voice rumbled, kicking her senses into overdrive.

"Good." She bit her lip before continuing. "I got a call from the adoption agency, asking me in for my interview." He was the last person she should tell, but something about him made her want to share her joy. And maybe, since the two of them weren't together, he was just the person to share her news.

His eyebrows jumped toward his hairline. "Really? That's great! I didn't know you'd decided to go that route."

She nodded.

"Congratulations."

"Thanks. I'm thrilled. How about you? How are you doing?"

He shrugged, and something about his movement made him seem lost. "Same old," he said. He took a drink of his coffee, his throat moving as he swallowed. "Trying to work out a few glitches here and there."

Glitches. The word reminded her of a recipe that didn't quite turn out as planned. Kind of like her life.

"Has work slowed down with the holidays approaching?" Lisa still couldn't believe she was sitting with Sander. And enjoying it. If she were smart, she'd let the man leave so they could continue with their lives on their own.

"Starting to. I don't have any new projects starting

until after the first of the year, but I'm trying to button down some supply issues before everyone leaves for their holiday celebrations."

"And you?" Her mouth had a mind of its own. Or maybe, it was connected to her heart. Regardless, it was time to admit she didn't want to up and leave.

He frowned. "Me?"

"What about your holiday celebrations?" She folded her arms on the table, leaning forward. His gaze was wary.

He shook his head, and a profound sadness filled her. As if on cue, "I'll Be Home for Christmas" began to play.

"I'll see everyone for Christmas Eve dinner at my house, and Kelsey, Trevor, and the triplets the next morning briefly, but other than that, nothing special."

She wasn't sure what she'd expected him to say, or how she imagined he'd celebrate, but somehow, what he described sounded...solitary. Before she could stop herself, she blurted, "Would you like to join me for the first night of Hanukkah? We're all going to my parents' house. Dinner, presents, lighting candles." *Oh God, what did I do?*

"I can't impose on you all."

Yet, all of a sudden, his presence didn't feel like an imposition. It felt necessary. Now that she'd invited him, she longed for his presence there. "It won't be an imposition at all. We're probably much more low-key than your Christmas celebrations, but my mom is an excellent cook."

He laughed. "Somehow, that doesn't surprise me."

Her cheeks heated. "Baking and cooking are totally different skills."

"Then you're a multitalented family."

"I'm serious," she said. "You're more than welcome. Besides, you haven't lived until you've tried our sweet potato latkes."

His eyes lit up. Seriously, the way to this man's heart was through his stomach. She swallowed. Not that she was trying to get to his heart.

"Okay, I'd love to join you all. Thank you."

She gave him her parents' address and watched him leave the coffee shop. Why was she doing this to herself? They both wanted different things. The best thing for both of them was to separate. Yet here she was, having invited him to celebrate with her, and she was looking forward to it!

What was *wrong* with her?

With a groan, she left the coffee shop and texted her mom to expect an extra guest. Nothing was going to come of it. She was being friendly. That was all.

Sander left the Emerald Ridge Café even more conflicted than when he'd arrived. Running into Lisa had brightened his day, and that was the problem. If her presence had made him feel better, then her absence was a major cause of his depression. How could one woman possess the ability to do that? And what did it mean for him going forward? Because they each knew that being together wasn't an option for either of them.

Just listening to her when she'd told him about her adoption meeting had driven that point home. If he'd been smart, he would have congratulated her and left. But no. He'd stayed, resulting in an invitation to celebrate Hanukkah with her. He scoffed. Here he was, not wanting to put much effort into commemorating his own holiday, and now he was going to celebrate hers too. He was a glutton for punishment.

Or maybe he needed the light she brought into his life. He'd never known anyone who could do that for him, whose very presence suddenly made his world right. Prior to meeting Lisa, he'd have laughed at anyone who suggested it to him. But now? He was a believer. And wasn't that just dandy. The one woman he couldn't have was the very woman who made him happy.

He huffed. Of course that would happen to him. So maybe, instead of fighting it, he should enjoy whatever random moments he could grab with her. Like in a coffee shop. Or on the street. At her parents' house.

That stopped him. He'd agreed to go to her family Hanukkah celebration, even though he wasn't Jewish and he wasn't her boyfriend. Would her family think it odd? He certainly did. But who the heck cared? It would be another chance to spend time with Lisa. They weren't a couple. And friendship was hard since they were attracted to each other. However, there was no chance of either of them acting on their attraction in the presence of others, especially her family. So maybe, this invite was the perfect way for them to spend time together as friends.

The fuzzy, roundabout logic appealed to him. He grabbed his phone and texted her.

> Thanks for the invitation.

That was bland. His fingers hovered over the keys, trying to figure out what else to say, but he drew a blank. The line between friend and lover, at least when it came to texting, was hard to find. So, he pressed Send and waited a few moments, wondering if she'd respond. When she did, he smiled.

> You're welcome. I'm glad you accepted.

> Does this mean we can be friends?

This time, her response took longer. Crap, was he pushing her too much? He hadn't meant to. He climbed into his truck, wondering what she'd say. If she'd say anything at all. She couldn't refuse his friendship, could she? Why would she have invited him otherwise?

When his phone buzzed as he sat at the traffic light, relief washed over him.

> Yes.

One little word. One woman. Her power over him astounded him. He shook his head.

As he drove home, another thought struck him. She'd mentioned gifts. He couldn't show up without something for her. And her family. He called his daughter.

"Help, what do I get Lisa for Hanukkah?"

"Hi, Dad." His daughter's amused voice irked him.

"Hi. Can you help me?"

"Does this mean the two of you are together?"

Damn, why had he called *her* of all people? "No, it means she invited me to her family Hanukkah celebration, and I can't show up empty-handed."

"Wait, for real?"

He should hang up. "No, I'm joking. April Fools, several month's early."

She gave a quiet laugh. "That's awesome. Ohhh, so that's why you don't want to spend Christmas with the family. You're going to spend it with her!"

Christmas with Lisa? No. Unless he returned the favor and invited her to join him for his holiday. He gulped. Was she expecting that from him? Hadn't even crossed his mind. Until now. Did this mean he needed two gifts? And what if she didn't want to come? He groaned.

He ground out her name between gritted teeth. "Kelsey."

"Yes?"

How did one word sound so innocent? "Can we stick to the topic? I need a gift for her for Hanukkah. Maybe her family too."

"And you're asking me..."

He rubbed his face. No way should he have called her, even if she was known for picking out great gifts. She had a knack of giving exactly what was needed, even if the recipient didn't know it at the time. "Momentary insanity. Can you help me anyway?"

Her laugh on the other end of the phone made his jaw ache.

"Of course. Were you thinking big, small, meaningful?"

His mind drew a blank. "I was invited less than ten minutes ago," he said. "I wasn't thinking anything."

"Okay, but what are you thinking now?"

Now? Right now he was thinking saying yes was the biggest mistake of his life. But that could be because of his daughter. Because seeing Lisa had gotten rid of the blues that had infected everything since the two of them had said their last goodbye. It was Kelsey who was the problem, now.

He tried to push away his frustration with her and focus on her question. Lisa didn't seem like the type of person who would want a huge gesture. She'd seemed ill at ease when he took her on their first date to the expensive restaurant. And she'd told him she couldn't afford the IVF treatments. So he certainly didn't want her uncomfortable with an expensive gift.

"Definitely not big, but I don't know if small is the way to go either."

"Then I think you should give her something meaningful," she said.

"But we're not dating."

"That's okay. Friends give each other special gifts all the time. What does she like? What are her interests?"

He thought for a moment. "She likes baking and cooking, but I wouldn't have any idea what to get her."

"You could go to the gift shop. They probably have holiday bundles that she might like."

Already-put-together bundles of random cooking supplies? "I don't think that's exactly meaningful, Kels."

"No, but it's of interest to her, which shows you're listening. Therefore, it would be meaningful."

True. He loved listening to Lisa talk. Her expressive face was like a window into her thought process. He'd never known a woman so easy to read.

Except she rarely talked about cooking or baking, unless they were doing it together. That's not to say she didn't mention it. She did, but they didn't have in-depth discussions about it. He chuckled. Probably because he honestly wouldn't know the difference between a teaspoon and a tablespoon without some help. Which meant he probably shouldn't get her something to bake or cook with. He wouldn't know where to start.

Still, he couldn't help thinking back to their rugelach baking—and the amazing sex afterward—at her house. His body heated just thinking about what they'd done together. Nope, probably not a good idea to get her anything that reminded her of what they'd done together. He shook his head to clear it and immediately cooled when he realized what she did talk about. *Kids*. She'd told him she had an appointment with the adoption agency. So she was serious about having a kid. If she were going to adopt a child, she probably didn't need any more clutter, especially the frivolous kind, which was what he'd end up getting her. Her house was small enough as it was.

His heart jumped. Her house was small. Even for one person.

That was it. He had a great idea for Lisa's Hanukkah gift.

"Kelsey, I've got it. Thanks for your help."

"I didn't do anything, Dad."
"I'll talk to you later."
He hung up and raced to his office to get started.

Chapter Nine

"Mom, where did you put the potato peeler?"

Lisa raced around her mom's kitchen, opening drawers and letting them slam shut when she couldn't find what she needed. The peace she usually found in the kitchen dissolved into thin air as she thought about Sander's arrival. She rummaged through her mother's kitchen tools, her heart pattering against her ribs as she searched in vain for the peeler. Where the heck was it?

"It's right where it always is," her mom said, leaning past her and pulling it out of the back of the utility drawer.

Lisa frowned. "I swear it wasn't there when I looked." She reached for the bag of potatoes, almost dropping it in her haste, before grabbing one and peeling in frantic strokes.

Her mom's cool hand on her arm made her slow down. "Where's the fire?" the older woman asked.

"We need to start making the latkes," Lisa said, angling her body so she could more easily get her work done. She wanted the scent of the latkes to entice him when he opened the door. "Sander's going to be here soon, and—"

"And he'll wait just like everyone else." Her mom's palm soothed her, tethering her to the moment.

Olivia and Molly raced into the kitchen.

"No running while we're cooking," her mom chided with a smile.

"Auntie Lisa, can we have some?"

Her nieces broke the spell, and Lisa laughed. "I haven't even started making them yet. And trust me, unlike sweet baked items, raw potatoes are gross. But as soon as the first batch are finished and cooled, you can be my tasters, okay?"

Nodding, the girls left, racewalking, but not running.

"Pretty soon you might have your own tasters," her mom said softly, lifting the frying pan onto the stove.

Lisa's chest tightened. "Let's not count on anything," she said. "I've had my heart broken too many times before." She'd told her parents and sister when she arrived earlier. They'd been thrilled for her, and their excitement added to her own. But it also made her nervous, as if by planning ahead, she was challenging the gods. She'd never been superstitious before trying to have children.

Now? She had a new understanding for women who had eaten random herbs back in the old days in order to increase their odds of having children. Not that she would do that. She was superstitious, not crazy.

Her mom gave her a squeeze and placed the bottle of oil next to the burner. "Is the adoption making you nervous, or is it Sander coming over?"

Her eyes prickled with tears as she sliced the onion.

She wished she could blame the offending vegetable, but lately, her emotions had been all over the place.

She blinked. "Is it that obvious?"

Her mom didn't answer, just gave her a sideways glance, and leaned against the counter, hands bracing her.

"Fine, it's obvious. A little of both, I guess. I'm so glad I invited him over, but I'm nervous too. I want us to be friends, but the boundaries... And I'm afraid to get my hopes up about the adoption until I have my meeting. And—"

The rest of what she was going to say was cut off by the bell ringing. Her eyes widened, and her heartbeat raced like the bubbles in a newly opened bottle of seltzer. She looked at her mom for help.

"He's here," the older woman said unnecessarily. "Relax, it will be fine."

Sure. Fine. No problem. Easy for *her* to say. With a deep breath, Lisa walked toward the front door, which already stood open. In the foyer of her parents' house stood her dad, her sister, her brother-in-law... and Sander.

Backlit by the setting sun, his features were cast into shadow. But the outlines were there—wide shoulders, long legs, powerful stance. If she were to trace him onto her heart, the image would be the same. Her stomach flip-flopped at the sound of his deep voice greeting her family. And then he stepped fully into the house, her dad shut the door, and she drank in all the details she'd missed. His longish blond hair was neatly combed, the ends curling against his neck. A deep rust-colored sweater made his hazel eyes warm. The wool accentuated his muscular chest, and his blue jeans hugged his thighs. She swallowed, imagining what the fitted denim did to his backside.

If she were to maintain the boundaries she mentioned to her mom, she had to stop thinking of him as sex on a stick. Even if he was. She groaned.

He smiled at her, a question in his eyes, while his cheeks widened and laugh lines bracketed his mouth. Pulling his hand away from her brother-in-law, he took two strides toward her.

"Happy Hanukkah, Lisa, Mrs. Schneider."

Lisa couldn't find her voice. Or her breath. What was going on? She'd been perfectly fine at the coffee shop. But seeing him in her parents' house, welcoming him to the family celebration. Something was different, and her body was taking a long time to adjust. Luckily, the pounding of her nieces' feet and her mother's, "Welcome, Sander, it's lovely to have you," covered her awkwardness. He handed a bouquet of flowers to her mom.

"These are for you," he said. "Thank you for the invitation."

Her mother sighed and buried her nose in the mixed bouquet of yellow roses and lilies. "You're welcome. Let me get them into some water."

And suddenly, the two of them were alone, the rest of the family reading some unspoken cue and melting into the background. She had to find her voice—and her breath—or risk looking crazy.

"Hi," she said. *Brilliant, Lisa.*

"Hello." His eyes glowed with warmth and a little humor, like he knew she was tongue-tied and found her amusing. "I like your dress."

She smoothed the blue fabric at her hips. "Thank you. Come inside?" She led him into the family room, where the rest of her family had resettled. Everyone's presence calmed her. Instead of sitting immediately, he walked around the room, looking at the myriad family photos her parents had hung over the years. She joined him, pointing out different people, laughing with him at some of her cringier moments—whoever had let her get that haircut with the sides shaved had no idea what they were doing—until they came to her wedding picture.

When her parents had insisted on keeping it up, Lisa had been against it, not wanting the reminder of her pain. But over the years, she'd managed to look at the photo with love and nostalgia. Now she was happy it was there. Something so beautiful shouldn't be erased.

Sander sobered. "You two look very happy," he said, his voice soft.

"We were."

"You're lucky—" Sander paused. "What's that amazing smell?"

"Latkes!" Olivia cried, running into the room. "Latkes are coming!"

Behind her, Lisa's mom entered carrying a platter of fresh-from-the-frying-pan potato pancakes. Lisa's sister followed with bowls of applesauce and sour cream.

"Olivia and Molly, let the grown-ups take first, please," David said.

Pouty faces greeted the announcement, until Lisa's dad winked. He grabbed two paper plates and placed two latkes on each one, with a spoonful of applesauce.

"Here you go," he said, handing the plates to the girls. "I'd never let my granddaughters miss out on the first latkes."

"Yay!" They rushed over to the corner where a play table was set up with two small chairs and dug in. The rest of the adults began to help themselves.

Sander leaned toward Lisa. "Do they taste as good as they smell?"

"Better." Talking about food calmed her, made her remember how much fun they had together. How much she enjoyed being around him.

Eyes wide, he reached for a plate and helped himself to a little of everything. Lisa loved how willing he was to try new things. Then again, he was a foodie, so of course he wanted to taste them. Once everyone had helped themselves, they all sat around the living room, chatting and eating.

"So, Sander, is this your first Hanukkah celebration?" Lisa's dad asked.

He nodded.

"Well, welcome."

"Thank you." He turned to Lisa's mother. "Ma'am, these are amazing."

Her mother blushed and nodded her head in acknowledgment. "I'm glad you like them."

He tipped his head and whispered, "Do you have these every Hanukkah?"

"Yes. Fried food celebrates the miracle of the oil."

She took a bite of her own latke, covered in sour cream. "Once the sun sets, we'll light the menorahs—the candelabras—say a few prayers, and then after dinner, we open presents."

"Small gifts," her mom interjected. "Except for the girls, of course. Their gifts are bigger."

"Of course," he said, his eyes twinkling.

Lisa swallowed. His gorgeous eyes sent shivers down her spine when he turned them on her. And today, he turned them on her often.

She'd never been this nervous around a man. Maybe, though, the jittery feeling wasn't nerves. Maybe it was more. Could that be?

"Grandma, you forgot about the dreidels and the donuts!" Molly, the oldest, ran over to her.

Lisa's mom covered her mouth. "Oh my goodness, I did!"

Both girls' faces drooped. "Really?" Olivia asked.

Lisa pulled them over to her side and gave them both a big hug. "You don't really think that could happen, sillies, do you? We could never forget about dreidels or donuts! In fact, I think the two of you might have the most important job of all today."

Their eyes widened. "Really? What?"

"You need to teach Sander how to play."

They walked over to him. "You don't know how to play dreidel?" Molly asked.

He glanced at Lisa before answering. "I do not."

"Come on," they said, grabbing him with their greasy hands. "We'll teach you."

Lisa grabbed the plate from his lap so it wouldn't

fall onto the floor. He rose, following them over to the other side of the living room.

Her heart melted at his acceptance of their messiness and their eagerness to teach him. And the fizzy feeling she'd had all day exploded. This definitely wasn't nerves. Her heart swelled, watching Sander's behavior with the two children she loved most in the world. Her nieces patted the floor next to them, and Sander folded himself onto the floor, crossing his long legs like a pretzel.

She couldn't bear to be away from the three of them. "Can I play too?" she asked, after cleaning up the remains of their snacks.

The girls looked at each other, giggled, and then shook their head no.

"Not yet, Auntie Lisa. You're too good. We have to show Sander first." Olivia got up and pulled on her arm until she bent down.

Cupping her hand around her mouth, Olivia whispered, "We don't want him to give up before he learns."

Lisa burst out laughing. Sander's quizzical gaze made her eyes water. She shook her head at him and wiped her eyes. When she'd calmed, replied, "Don't worry. You're in good hands."

The girls were patient as they showed him each Hebrew letter on the dreidel, quizzing him on their meanings until he knew what to do for each letter. Next, they taught him how to spin the wooden top. He got the hang of that pretty quickly, his long fingers sending the dreidel into long spins that had the girls oohing and aahing. Finally, they decided he was ready to play. And the more involved he got with them, the faster her heart beat.

"Okay, Auntie Lisa, *now* you can sit with us," Molly said.

Exchanging a knowing look with her own sister—both remembering how bossy they'd been as little girls—she sat with the three of them, her knees touching Sander's. Heat zipped from him to her.

"Youngest goes first," Olivia cried.

Sander glanced at Lisa and laughed. "Pretty sure she's taking control of the entire game," he whispered.

With his face this close to hers, all she wanted to do was kiss him. "You know it," Lisa responded. They exchanged a look filled with want, before she turned away.

They all placed one penny into the center, joining the ten that were already there.

Olivia spun the dreidel and it landed on the letter Hay. She crowed and grabbed half of the pennies in the center for herself.

Next it was Molly's turn. After everyone contributed one penny, she spun a Gimmel. She jumped up and down with glee.

"Molly calm down," her mom called from across the room. "Nobody likes a sore winner."

With a sheepish grin, she sank back down and took all of the pennies in the center.

Sander went next, spinning a Shin. "I put one penny in, right?" he asked.

The smiles on the girls faces were just as bright as they'd been when they won their pennies. "You got it!"

And again, everyone put a penny into the middle and Lisa spun, also spinning a Gimmel. With a quick grin at Sander, she took the pennies from the center.

The four of them continued the game until Sander had run out of all his pennies. He groaned and placed his head in his hands.

The girls rushed over and gave him a hug. "It's okay, you did a good job," Olivia said.

Molly nodded, before handing him her pennies. "Here, you can have mine."

Lisa's heart melted. He hugged them back, glancing past them at Lisa, and refused the pennies.

She'd read his expression and knew he was only faking his dismay to show the girls how into the game he was. He was so good with kids. Her throat thickened. He must have been an amazing dad. Kelsey was one lucky young woman.

She joined in the conversation. "It's so sweet of you to offer your pennies," she said. "But you should keep them."

The look of relief that passed over Molly's face almost made Lisa laugh. And from the reddish hue creeping along Sander's neck, she suspected he felt the same way. The girls took their winnings and raced over to their parents. Sander's shoulders shook with silent laughter.

"They're adorable," he murmured, his hazel eyes crinkling with merriment. "But I didn't mean to panic them. I thought they'd like seeing me lose."

"Oh, I'm sure they did." She turned toward her sister and brother-in-law, just in time to see the girls bragging. She pointed. "See, they're quite proud of themselves. But they didn't want you to be sad."

Sander grasped her hand and pulled her to her feet. But instead of letting go, he held on. She stood next to him, heart pounding. Barely aware of anything but the man next to her, she and Sander joined the adults on the other side of the room as Lisa's dad called, "Dinner is ready." He directed his next words to the girls. "Go wash your hands, please."

Lisa laughed. "Just them? You're okay if we have dirty hands?"

He wrapped his arm around her shoulders. "No, I just assumed I had less control over you. They're still young enough to listen to me." He planted a kiss on her forehead and returned to the kitchen.

Lisa led Sander into the dining room. He paused in the doorway and then looked around. "Are you expecting more people?"

Lisa's mom laughed. "Welcome to our Jewish home, where fear of someone possibly starving creates feasts like this one!"

Lisa pointed out the different dishes. "Eggplant salad, spinach salad, couscous, Moroccan sweet potatoes, roast goose with chestnut and apple stuffing, and Moroccan carrot salad."

He groaned. "I'm never going to leave."

Lisa's heartbeat quickened, and she bit her lip. Her fingers itched to whip out an apron and cook up another meal, and another after that. Anything to make him stay. But her head knew better. Bribing him with food wouldn't change his mind, and it would diminish her in the process. She shook her head to clear it of any fantasy she might have and settled in at the table.

Conversation flowed, interspersed with peals of laughter from her nieces, groans of approval from Sander, and a few carefully crafted pointed questions from her dad. Each time he asked Sander about his family's traditions or his knowledge of Jewish history, Lisa's sister and brother-in-law glanced at Lisa, as if ready to step in if Sander needed defending.

Her chest warmed at the support, despite how unnecessary it was. Sander was her friend. While she wished things could be different between them, she knew he would never be more than that. Additionally, even if somehow the stars aligned and all the roadblocks faded away, she was well past the age where she needed her parents' permission to date someone.

Sander handled everything better than she'd have anticipated.

"I've never celebrated Hanukkah before," he responded when her dad asked if he had. "But my cousin, Shane, has talked about what a beautiful holiday it is." He sat back, resting one arm on the back of Lisa's chair, the other on his stomach. "His fiancée, Naomi, is Jewish."

Lisa inhaled. "I love Naomi," she said. "Don't ask me why I didn't make the Fortune connection there."

"If he had told me how amazing the food is, let me tell you, I'd have celebrated this long ago. Mr. and Mrs. Schneider, dinner was amazing."

Lisa's mom glanced at her for a moment before answering, her eyes full of love. "I'm so glad you enjoyed it. As usual, we have leftovers, so if you'd like to take anything home with you, you're welcome to do so."

David checked out the window. "It's getting dark," he said. "Let's help Grandma clear the table, and then I think it's time to light the candles."

Two chairs scraped against the dining room floor as Molly and Olivia raced to help their grandmother. Lisa withheld a laugh, even as she winced at the scratches her nieces were obviously creating. As her sister corralled the girls and convinced them to behave, the other adults rose and made short work of the dirty dishes. Even Sander helped, and Lisa could practically see the points he was racking up with her family. She pulled her menorah out of the bag, as well as the box of candles she'd brought, and placed it on the credenza below the living room window, where everyone else's menorahs sat.

She and Jordan had received the menorah as a wedding gift. Each of the nine branches resembled narcissus branches, with leaves and pearl stones for flowers. Jordan had complained it was a little "girlie" for him, but Lisa thought it was breathtaking. Along with hers, her parents' silver one sat in the center, and her sister and brother-in-law's was situated on the other end. Even the girls brought their own. By the time they were all lit, the lights would glow. Sander joined her, and she explained what she was doing as she removed candles from the box.

"Since it's the first night of Hanukkah, we use two candles. This one is the shamash, or helper candle that lights all the others." She set it in the center. "And this one is for the first night." She placed it all the way in the branch farthest to the right.

He stood behind her, the warmth of his body flooding through her as everyone else prepared their menorahs as well. Each candelabra was different and fit the personalities of the owners. Her parents was an ornate silver one they'd purchased in Israel. Her sister and brother-in-law's was also a wedding gift, made of bronze with different colored jewels. And the girls had their own—a unicorn, complete with glitter and rainbow streamers, the candles placed along the animal's back.

As they lit the candles and chanted the prayers, Sander's hands cupped Lisa's shoulders. Her eyes watered. Touched by the moment and the intimate gesture, she wished they could be together, to celebrate both their holidays as a family. Her throat thickened as she realized, despite all her attempts to deny it, she'd fallen in love with him. She shut her eyes, trying to push away the feeling or trap it deep down where she'd never notice it. Hoping not to draw notice to herself, she brushed away a few tears that threatened to overflow.

His voice whispered in her ear. "Are you all right?"

She swallowed the lump in her throat and nodded, refusing to speak the lie or to turn and face him.

Her niece tugged on her hand, and she looked down, blinking.

"Auntie Lisa," Molly whispered in a voice that wasn't a whisper at all. "I didn't get anything for Mr.... him." Her lip trembled as she shuffled from one foot to the other.

Lisa knelt down and ran a gentle finger beneath her lower lashes, where tears hung in the balance, just as they had for her. She gave her niece a hug. "That's okay, sweetheart. He isn't expecting one from you."

"But I don't want him to feel bad," she said. "He was so nice when we played dreidel together."

Sander hovered in the background, and she wondered what he thought of the little girl. As if reading her mind, he knelt down next to them.

"You know what?" he asked.

Molly looked at him, not saying a word.

"I have a problem that maybe you can help me with. I have a refrigerator—" he pointed at the one in the Schneiders' kitchen "—just like that one. But it's completely bare."

She followed his outstretched arm to where he pointed.

"Bare?" she asked. Her sister came over and looked at the fridge as well.

"Yep. Bare. It doesn't have a single picture on it."

Molly's eyes widened. Olivia gaped and covered her mouth.

Lisa's insides melted once again. At this rate, she'd be a pile of goo by the end of the evening.

"Can we draw you some pictures to hang up when you get home?" The girls' voices wove together, increasing in volume.

Sander nodded. "I'd love that."

Like magic, Molly's tears dried up, and her lips curved in a smile. Olivia took her hand and they ran back to the play table, where Lisa's mom always kept crayons and paper.

Lisa's sister and mother watched the girls race away. They laughed. "Guess that gives us time to serve dessert before presents," they said.

"I think presents might be the only thing better than sugary treats," Lisa's dad chimed in.

Sander rose to his feet and pulled Lisa up with him. As everyone busied themselves setting out dessert, she squeezed his hand.

"That was very sweet of you," she said.

"I'm a girl dad." He shrugged as if that explained everything away.

It kind of did. He was already a dad, knew exactly what to do in fatherly situations. He just didn't want to start over with *her*. Lisa's stomach twisted, like someone was wringing out a wet washcloth. Eating was useless. Even the delicious dinner sat like a lump in her belly. She joined everyone at the table for donuts, their dessert of choice for a holiday celebrating the miracle of oil. But she only picked at the sugary sweet. A worried glance from Sander made her shake her head. As she turned, she caught the look exchanged between her mom and sister. They wouldn't say anything now, but she'd bet her nieces' dreidel winnings they'd confront her later.

She didn't want to talk to them about it. She had no one but herself to blame. Inviting Sander had been a mistake. Lisa paused. Not a mistake, exactly. He fit into her family like he was meant to be. But that was the problem. Because he wasn't meant to be—with her or with them. And every time she thought she could handle a simple friendship, she was proven wrong. Because she loved him. Loved every part of him and would give anything to be with him forever. She clenched her hands beneath the table. Exactly how many times did she need to see how hard just being friends with Sander was going to be before she believed it?

Finally, when the donuts were eaten and the dishes were cleared, her dad rose, eyes gleaming. "Who's ready for presents?"

Lisa gave herself a mental shake. No matter how she might feel, she didn't want to do anything to ruin the experience for her nieces. Or for the rest of the family.

Against the squeals of the two little girls, all the adults moved into the living room, grabbing the blue, silver, and white packages they'd brought in upon arrival. The chaos of noise and unwrapping and hugs lightened Lisa's mood. She couldn't help but share in their excitement, and she eagerly watched as her nieces opened the baking sets she'd bought them.

"Can we cook with you?" they asked, running over and squeezing her tight.

"Of course! That's why I bought them. I'll talk to Mommy, and we'll set a date." She looked over at her sister, and when the girls had moved on to their next gifts, she handed her sister and brother-in-law their card.

Sara's eyes lit up. "Babysitting! Yay!"

Lisa laughed. "We'll combine the two events so the two of you can have a weekend to yourselves."

Her sister handed her a card as well. "There's an

adorable store with kid furniture. I thought you might like to pick out some pieces once you get further along in the adoption process."

Lisa looked down at the Mini Me Furniture logo, her hand shaking. "I can't wait. Thank you!"

Sander cleared his throat. "Speaking of adoption..." He handed her a gift bag. "Happy Hanukkah."

Her heart fluttered. Frowning, she opened the bag and pulled out a rolled piece of paper. She unraveled it and gasped. Tears filled her eyes. Looking up at him, she flung herself into his arms. His solid warmth made her cry harder, and around her, everyone stopped their celebrations. Despite the audience, all she could do was let her emotions wash over her. She disappeared into the scratchy softness of his wool sweater, his heartbeat steady against her ear. Her throat ached. How could one man be so perfect and yet so out of reach? Finally she calmed, sniffling and wiping the tears from her face.

She pulled back, her face warm with embarrassment over her emotional display. But she couldn't stop staring at the man who had given her the most perfect present of all.

He leaned down and whispered in her ear, "Were those good tears or bad ones?"

Flashing him a watery smile, she said, "Good ones."

Turning to her family, she brought the paper with her and flattened it out in front of her. "He—"

She swallowed, unable to continue without bursting into tears again. Taking a deep breath, she spoke, her voice shaky. "He gave me plans to expand and adapt my house for when I adopt a child."

Her parents and sister gasped, their faces flushing with color. "Oh, Sander, how perfect," Lisa's mom said.

"Your house is kind of small," Sara agreed.

Everyone leaned over the plans and examined them, as Sander explained how she could move a few walls, expand closets and bathrooms, while keeping the same footprint of the house. He'd added built-in storage to her living room and even provided an optional kitchen expansion, which would require bumping out the back wall to give her more room. Visions of cooking and baking and hosting holiday dinners danced before her eyes.

Lisa listened as he fully explained everything he'd drafted. She stared at the plans he'd drawn up, her fingers pressed against the edge of the paper. She had a crazy urge to whisk the plans away from everyone, to pore over them herself, in private. As if leaving them here for everyone to see would diminish them in some way.

Questions rattled around in her brain, bursting to be asked, but she stifled all of them. If she uttered even one, she'd never be able to stop. She was afraid of getting carried away, of requiring more of him than he was prepared to give. She was afraid of telling him she loved him.

He'd picked the one thing only he could give her, and she ached at how he'd never be able to share the results. It was the most unselfish gift he could have chosen, something to help her achieve her dream of motherhood.

A dream he didn't want to be a part of. And that was why she had to remain silent.

Her fingers froze, and she pressed them harder against the plans, whitening their tips. Her heart shattered, and as she stared at the rendering, the lines and angles dissolved like a kaleidoscope, until in her mind's eye, nothing remained but a blank sheet of paper. Destroyed, like her dreams and her heart. She met his gaze, and even his features were a blur.

When the tears poured from her eyes, his eyes narrowed, and his throat moved as he swallowed.

"Lisa?" His voice deepened with concern. "Did I do something wrong?"

How could he possibly think that?

"Wrong? I...no...you..." She couldn't do this here. Not with all eyes on her. With her heart pounding against her ribs, she fled the room, escaped the house, and burst onto the front porch. The cool air fanned her cheeks. Chest heaving, she gulped in huge swallows of air, shuddering as the heat rolled off her body and cooled instantly. Her knees buckled and she struggled to remain standing.

The door snicked open and heavy footsteps creaked across the porch. Sander's large body enveloped her, even though he remained inches away. She longed for him to hold her, and after a brief moment, he drew her toward him like a magnet, wrapped his arms around her, and held her tight. His strength was the only thing keeping her upright.

Her eyes and throat burned and her thoughts jumbled in her head.

"I..." She didn't know how to continue. "You..." The tears she'd tried so hard to hold back spilled over.

Sander held her, rubbing her back and remaining blessedly silent. When she finally gained control, she stepped back and raised her gaze to his.

The stricken look on his face ravaged her with guilt.

"What did I do?" His face was solemn, eyes filled with concern.

His voice washed over her, making her ache even more. "You created the most amazing gift I've ever received." She broke his gaze, swallowed, and continued. "You studied my house when you were there, didn't you?"

"It's a hazard of the trade, even if ranches are my specialty. But I didn't mean for it to be a bad thing. I never intended to make you cry."

His expression was so pained, Lisa would have laughed if she thought she could pull it off without bursting into tears again. Men usually looked uncomfortable when women cried, and Sander was no exception.

She shook her head. "No, it's not bad at all. It's the most generous gift... It's incredible."

"*That's* why you're crying?" Sander's disbelief made his eyebrows reach his hairline.

She nodded. "No one has ever done something so unselfish for me. Ever."

He exhaled. The look of relief on his face pierced her. This man, this amazing man, had done something so selfless and she'd caused him to doubt himself.

Stepping forward, she reached up and took his face

in her hands. His skin was warm against her palms. She caressed his cheeks before pulling him down for a kiss. Passion ignited and everything disappeared except for this one exquisite man. Hungrily, she tried to put into her kiss what she'd been unable to convey with words.

He wrapped his arms around her and held her so close, she could feel his heart pound against hers.

"Let's get out of here," she whispered against his mouth.

His gaze cloudy with desire, he frowned as he traced her mouth with his thumb. "But it's your family's Hanukkah celebration," he said. "I don't want to offend them."

She shook her head. "They won't miss us. Trust me."

He looked behind him at the closed door and then back at her.

"My place?"

Her heart sped up and the overwhelming emotion she'd felt moments before shifted to pure excitement.

"Yes."

And without another word, he scooped her up in his arms and carried her to his truck.

Chapter Ten

In a flurry of roaming hands and tugged clothes and mouths, Sander pulled Lisa into his house. He kept hold of her as they kissed their way into his living room.

"I want you right here, right now," he murmured against her warm neck.

"Yes," she whispered. "Yes."

Heart pounding, he turned her around and unzipped her dress, his mouth trailing the zipper and raining kisses down her spine.

"As gorgeous as you looked in this dress, I've been aching to get you out of it," he said as he drew it down over her hips.

She stepped out of it, then pulled his sweater up over his head. "Not as much as I've wanted to do the same to you," she replied.

And then she ran her hands all around his chest and he couldn't breathe. His limbs moved on autopilot, shucking his boots and jeans, but his attention was on Lisa.

Beautiful Lisa with her creamy skin, luscious breasts, long legs.

"Wait." His voice was hoarse with need, and he held

her away from him, hating the space but needing a moment of clarity.

Leaving her where she was, he rushed into his bedroom, returning a moment later with a condom. She nodded, and he tossed it onto the coffee table, before pulling her into his arms and kissing her senseless.

Their breaths quickened as they kissed and stroked each other, disappearing into a haze of desire that built with every second that passed.

When he could no longer stand it, he grabbed a blanket from the couch, along with a couple of throw pillows. Lisa spread them on the rug, and the two of them lowered themselves onto the floor.

He stared into her eyes, caressing her cheek. "You're so beautiful," he said. "I haven't been able to take my eyes off you this entire evening."

She smiled, her eyes shining. "I haven't been able to catch my breath since you walked in the door."

He kissed her again, tasting her sweetness. As she leaned against him, his body hardened. Not breaking contact with her, he reached blindly for the foil packet on the table.

"Let me," she said. Before he had a chance to react, she'd torn open the packet and slipped it on him.

"I need you now," he whispered, rolling with her and rising above her.

When she nodded, he penetrated her, easing himself in and watching her reaction.

She felt so good. He groaned, and she arched beneath him.

"Yes," she said. "Yes."

Together they found their rhythm, reaching higher and higher until with a last thrust, she cried out. Her muscles tightened around him, and with a shout, he crashed over the edge.

Their breaths rasped as their sweat-slicked bodies moved as one. He held her tight against him, not wanting the slightest space to come between them. Her heart beat in time with his, and his eyes prickled in amazement at how in tune they were with one another.

As their pulses returned to normal and their skin cooled, he pulled the blanket around them.

She nuzzled against his chest. "That was so wonderful, I almost didn't notice that we're on the floor."

He huffed a laugh. "Yeah, I might be too old to do this here again."

Looking at him askance, she grinned. "Too old? Never."

"Ha, talk to me tomorrow."

They stayed where they were, nestled in the blanket and pillows, until finally he rose up on an elbow. "I have to move, but I don't want to ruin this," he said, pointing to their slice of home.

Nodding, she rose, took his hand and walked with him to the bedroom.

"Aah," he sighed as they sank onto the mattress. "This is so much more comfortable."

She giggled and nuzzled his neck, her hands trailing lazy circles across his chest.

"If you keep doing this, we're going to need another condom," he whispered in her ear.

"Oh, I think I sense a challenge."

* * *

The next morning, Lisa awoke to sun slanting across the sheets from the wrong direction. Squinting, she opened her eyes and memories of last night fell into place, like slides in a photo carousel. Sander's kisses. Sander's touch. Sander's heat.

She turned, his body next to her in bed, one arm slung across her waist.

"Hello, beautiful," he murmured.

"You're awake."

"I don't want to miss any time with you."

She couldn't help the warmth his words and touch and very presence ignited. Turning to him, she met his lips with hers, reveling in the joy of waking up with someone. Morning kisses turned into more, and an hour later, they lay next to each other, spent, satiated, and hungry.

Her stomach rumbled. At last, she was hungry.

"Stay? I'll go make breakfast," Sander said.

She had nothing pressing she had to accomplish, and she nodded, admiring his sexy backside as he strode across the room completely naked.

By the time she'd climbed out of bed, donned one of his shirts, and made it into the kitchen after washing up, the aroma of bacon, eggs, and toast almost brought her to her knees. That and the man standing at the stove in only a pair of jeans, his wide chest on display for her to… Oh, what did she want to do first?

Everything.

"Like what you see?" he asked with a wink.

"Mmm-hmm." She wrapped her arms around him.

"Dad?"

The female call made her jump back, and before she could hide or think or do anything, a young woman with a baby strapped to her front and another two in a stroller entered the kitchen.

"Hi, I— Oh!" The woman turned away, hand over her eyes. "I'm so sorry."

"Hello, Kelsey. This is Lisa. Lisa, my daughter, Kelsey."

Lisa couldn't stop staring at the triplets, which gave her something to think about other than how she was meeting Sander's daughter for the first time in barely any clothes. The babies were adorable, with beautiful brown skin and adorable curls.

"Hi, Kelsey, nice to meet you."

"I swear, I knocked," Kelsey said.

"Now you know how I felt that one time I walked in on you and Trevor—"

"Okay, not having that discussion," Kelsey cried, holding up a hand as if she could physically stop the words. "I just came to see if you wanted to join me at the gingerbread house contest at the community center, but clearly, you've got other plans."

Sander brought the food he'd cooked to the counter.

"Actually, other than sitting down for breakfast, we hadn't actually set our plans. Lisa?"

A chance to spend time with Sander?

Yes, please!

Not to mention those adorable babies.

"I'd love to." She smiled at Kelsey. "Your babies are so cute."

Kelsey gave her a smile. "Thank you. It's nice to finally meet you. I hear you make amazing challah."

Lisa smiled before sitting down to eat.

"Join us?" Sander asked.

Kelsey shook her head. "With these three, I ate hours ago. How about we meet at the center in like forty-five minutes?"

"Sure thing," Sander said. "See you then." He walked Kelsey out and returned quickly to the kitchen.

"Sorry about that," he said.

Lisa laughed. "It could have been much worse."

"That's very true," he agreed.

After they finished eating and stopped at Lisa's house for a change of clothing, Sander drove them into town.

"Have you ever been to this?" he asked as he pulled into a parking space and shoved his hat on his head.

She fixed a strand of his hair that got mussed by the hat before taking his offered hand and walking with him into the center.

"Nope, although some of my students were talking about it."

Sander tipped his chin up. "There she is."

Once again, Kelsey stood with a baby strapped to her front and two in the stroller. She'd positioned herself off to the side, out of the way of the scores of people streaming in and out of the main hall.

"Hey, Dad. Lisa." She looked around, her auburn hair swinging around her shoulders. "This place is packed."

Lisa nodded. "I had no idea this contest was so popular." She leaned down to the babies in the stroller. "They're so sweet," she said. "You must have your hands full." She tried to stop the wistfulness from creeping into her voice, but she suspected she was unsuccessful.

"We do, but it's fun," Kesley said.

"Let's go on in," Sander said, ushering everyone toward the door as he chucked the baby against Kelsey's chest under her chin.

Inside the main hall, tables lined the perimeter and filled the center, creating aisles for the public to walk.

"That one is massive," Lisa cried, pointing to a castle that took up an entire corner of the room.

It had turrets made of gumdrops, chocolate sliding doors, and even stained glass windows made of colorful hard candies.

Sander spent time studying it from all angles. "I realize I'm a ranch architect, but in my next life, I want to design these," he said, his voice filled with awe.

"Or when you retire?" Lisa asked, one eyebrow raised.

"Maybe," he said.

Kelsey laughed. "You just want to eat your mistakes."

"Can't say I object to that plan." He knocked her with his shoulder.

Lisa watched the two of them interact. Clearly, they got along, and as she suspected from when she'd witnessed Sander with her nieces, he was a great dad.

As they wandered through the exhibit, Lisa divided her attention between watching the babies and admiring the creative gingerbread houses. By the time they reached the end of the exhibit, she was completely overwhelmed.

"How in the world am I supposed to choose my favorite?" she asked. "They're all so creative."

Kelsey agreed. "I think I have to vote for the castle, though, on sheer size alone. Plus, those stained glass windows were gorgeous."

"Good point," Lisa said. "Although I also liked the greenhouse with the orchids made from M&Ms."

"How about you, James?" Sander asked as he played with the little boy in the stroller. "Which was your favorite?"

James cooed and gave a gummy grin.

"I agree," Sander said. "The castle has to be the winner."

Lisa's heart melted and she gave Sander a tender smile. Arm in arm, they walked out of the main hall.

"S'mores," Sander said, pointing to a sign. "Who wants s'mores?"

"How can you possibly be hungry?" Lisa asked. "We only ate breakfast a couple of hours ago."

He leaned down to whisper in her ear, "We burned a lot of calories last night…and this morning…"

Lisa's face heated and she turned away.

"Uncle Sander!"

A male voice made the three adults stop, and Lisa wondered if she was destined to run into Sander's entire family at the most inopportune moments.

"Harris, Sofia, kids, hi." He turned to Lisa. "This

is my nephew, his wife, and her two kids, Kaitlin and Jackson. This is Lisa Bergen."

Everyone said hello, and Lisa got the distinct impression they were more curious about her than they were about the displays inside.

"We were just about to get s'mores," Kelsey said. "Join us?"

As a group, they headed toward the snack area, ordered s'mores and miraculously found enough space to sit together.

"The gingerbread exhibit is fantastic," Lisa said to the newcomers. "Be prepared to have a really tough time casting your votes."

The kids craned their necks to see inside the hall.

"I heard there was a robot," Jackson said.

Sander nodded. "Yup, it was pretty cool."

Just then, the babies started fussing.

"Well, that's my cue," Kelsey said. She cleaned up her mess and rose. "Dad, this was fun, and, Lisa, it was great meeting you. I hope to see you around more. Harris, Sofia, have fun in there." She gave everyone hugs and left.

Sander turned to Lisa. "We should probably get going too."

"Nice to meet all of you," Lisa said as she rose from the table. "Enjoy the exhibit."

Sander ushered Lisa out the door and stopped in front of his truck. "I have a little work I need to get done, but want to meet for dinner later?"

Lisa nodded. "I need to check in with my family so

they know I'm alive and do a few things as well. How about you come to my house and I'll cook?"

His eyes gleamed. "I'll never turn down your food."

Over the next few days, Lisa and Sander fell into a routine. Some days they spent apart getting work and errands done. Others, they went for a drive or found a fun holiday activity to do. But their breakfasts and dinners together were Lisa's favorite times.

It was while she was cooking—after lighting the menorah each night with Sander by her side—that they had some of their best conversations. She talked about her dream vacation to Greece and Turkey, and he told her how he wanted to tour all the ballparks in the United States. She regaled him with some of the funnier Hanukkah gifts she'd received, and he taught her some of his favorite Christmas traditions. And every day she fell more in love with him.

Sander sat across Lisa's tiny kitchen table and reached for her hand. The past few days with her had been better than he'd ever experienced. For the first time in as long as he could remember, he had a partner, someone he could count on. And rather than needing space, or feeling smothered, he relished every second with her.

"So what should we do today?" he asked. "I have about an hour or two of work I need to get done, but then I'm completely free."

"I have some papers to grade, but like you, I'm open. Any last-minute shopping you want to do?"

He nodded. "I could always pick up an extra toy or

two for the babies." He grinned. "I plan to spoil them rotten."

"I can tell." Her eyes softened and he wanted to jump over the table and wrap her up and never let her go. He loved that expression on her face.

"So that's the plan, then," he said. "I'll pick you up when I'm finished and we'll spend the day shopping."

"Like I'd ever turn that down," she said.

He rose, picked up their plates, and leaned down to kiss her. "I'd never turn you down either," he murmured against her lips.

Reluctantly, he pulled away, but not before grabbing a lock of her silky hair and letting it slide through his fingers. And then, before he could change his mind, he returned home and sat down to work for a couple hours.

After pressing Send on his last email, he shoved away from his desk, stretched, and changed his clothes before rushing back to Lisa's house. He'd never been so excited to battle the holiday crowds.

Because he'd do anything, go anywhere, as long as she was with him.

"Where to first?" he asked after he'd kissed her hello and helped her into his truck.

"Let's go to the Emerald Ridge Toy Store," she said. "I don't want to deprive those adorable babies of any Christmas gifts."

He drove to the boutique toy store, found a parking spot two blocks away, and the two of them held hands all the way into the store.

Mass chaos erupted. Wailing toddlers, impatient

parents, and noisy toys drowned out the holiday music piped in from the speakers.

"Maybe this isn't such a good idea," he muttered as they attempted to push their way farther into the store.

"Ouch!" he cried out as a toddler belted him with a random toy.

"Sorry," his mother said with an apologetic smile.

He tried to scan the store over everyone's heads in an effort to find the least crowded area, but there wasn't one.

"This will teach me to buy toys right before Christmas," he muttered. "Ew," he said, looking down at his hand that was now covered in someone's drool.

Lisa laughed and handed him a tissue from her purse. "It's definitely an adventure," she said with a smile.

He shook his head. "I don't miss this at all."

Lisa turned away for a moment. When she turned back, she held up her phone. "I have to take this call. I'm going outside, but will be right back."

He sighed. He hadn't even heard her phone ring. "I'm going to see if there's anything in here I can find, otherwise, I'll give up and meet you outside."

Nodding, she walked off. He had more than half a mind to follow her, to hell with the presents, but then he'd have to come back here again. Shuddering, he grabbed a container of wooden blocks and headed to the checkout counter. Ten minutes later, he finally made it outside.

"Thank God," he said as he reached Lisa. "That was awful."

She held up a finger, and he grimaced, mouthed, "Sorry," and waited for her to finish her phone call. Her joyful expression when she hung up filled him with warmth.

"That was the adoption agency confirming my appointment with them." Energy reverberated off her, practically making her vibrate. "I'm so excited for this interview," she said, taking his hand.

He nodded. "I'm glad it's working out for you," he said.

"Do you want to go with me?" she asked.

He shuddered, still reeling from the chaos in the toy store.

"Never mind," she said, her voice quiet. "Forget I said anything."

He squeezed her hand. "It's probably better you go yourself. That way, you're in complete control of the situation. But you can tell me all about it afterward."

"Yeah, probably," she said, but her voice was quiet. Too quiet.

"Lis, what's going through that gorgeous brain of yours?"

"So many things," she said. She wouldn't look at him.

"Like..."

She shrugged, and his heart dropped.

"Lisa, talk to me." He led her back to his truck, where they'd have privacy.

"What are we doing, Sander?"

He knew she didn't mean right this minute, and as

much as he wished she did, he couldn't respond with a flip answer. He cared too much about her.

"To be honest, I'm not sure," he said, grasping her hand and pressing it to his lips. "But whatever we're doing, I like it. Don't you?"

She nodded, her gaze troubled. "Too much."

"What's that mean? I thought we were friends."

"I thought we could be. But, Sander, it's too hard." She gulped. "This week has been everything I've ever wanted and more. But I can't think about anyone else when I'm around you. All I want to do is disappear into your life when we're together, and that's not fair to either of us. We set boundaries for a reason, but each time we're together, I want so much more from you."

"Maybe we just need more time," he said, his voice raspy with emotion.

"Time is exactly what I don't have, Sander." She shook her head. "I want you to want a baby as much as I do, and I can't force that on you. Our dreams are too different. Even inside the toy store, all you wanted was to escape, and all I could think about was how lucky all those parents were. You deserve to have the life you want, without sacrificing it for anyone. You've certainly waited long enough. But I want my dreams as well, and I've put them on hold for too long. Those dreams don't mesh."

"That doesn't mean we can't be—" he shrugged "—whatever this has been."

She shook her head. "I'm afraid if we continue on this path we're on, that boundary we've set is going to blur, or we're going to resent each other, and somehow, I'm going to hurt you."

Sander's body sagged against the driver's seat. "Lisa." He leaned toward her. "What about you? The last thing I want to do is hurt you."

She gave a hollow laugh. "I'm already hurt. From loss, from denial, from not being able to be with the one man who I most want to be with."

He started to speak, but she held up a hand.

"You are possibly the kindest man I've ever known. Certainly the most generous. You stepped in and devoted your life to raising your daughter. Put your life on hold to raise your nieces and nephews. Heck, you even helped raise your housekeeper's son. I'm afraid if we stay together, even as friends, you're going to sacrifice your needs for me, and I couldn't live with myself if that happened. I don't ever want to be the cause of you doing something, like staying in a crowded toy store, that isn't your choice."

He smacked his hands against the steering wheel. "You got all that from one trip to the store? Or from my turning down your invitation to join you at the adoption interview? I think you're reading too much into things."

She shook her head. "It's more than the store, more than your reaction to my invitation to the adoption agency, even more than your thoughtful architectural plan. It's everything. I've got a broken heart. And I don't want to be the one to break yours too."

Silence stretched between them, interrupted only by the sound of the motor turning over as he pulled out of the parking spot. Finally, Sander spoke.

"I guess that's it, then. I guess we really have to let each other go."

She nodded. The second he pulled into her driveway, even before he'd fully turned off his truck, she'd unbuckled her seat belt and reached for the door.

"Lisa…"

After an endless silence, Sander touched her shoulder. And without another word, Lisa climbed out of the truck and walked away from him.

Chapter Eleven

Misery burned through Sander's veins, making every waking moment almost too painful to bear. This desolation was different from anything he'd felt before. Loss had become part of his life, whether it was Kelsey's mother, his brother and sister-in-law, or his housekeeper's son. When he'd lost Lani, he'd been young and overwhelmed. And while his feelings for her originally had been strong, they were more like a firework—white-hot, flashy, and quick to blow out. He suspected lots of people in the throes of first love felt this way. However, once he saw her for who she truly was, and how she'd so easily walked away from her child, whatever last vestige of love he'd had for her fizzled.

His love for his children—and he considered his nieces and nephews, and even Linc, his children—was deeper, more textured. Linc's death had crushed him, but still, there was a separation between him and the young man he'd tried to be a "dad figure" to. While he doubted he'd ever get over the pain of Linc's violent death, it was a different kind of love than what he felt for Lisa.

It was also a different kind of pain.

He and Lisa were officially over, and he ached with the injustice of it all. Sure, there was a rational side of his brain that understood, and probably had from the beginning, that a platonic friendship between two people who shared such a strong chemistry and potent visceral connection was probably not going to work. But he'd ignored the rational side of his brain, taken as he was by Lisa. If only there was a way to maintain some sort of relationship with her. Except they'd tried that, multiple times, and failed miserably. He couldn't get Lisa's hurt expression out of his head.

No wonder he hadn't recognized his feelings for Lisa. He'd never felt them before. How could he have fallen for the one woman who was so wrong for him? His chest hurt, the weight of his misery constricting his lungs and making it impossible to breathe.

He *loved* her. The knowledge had hit him in the middle of the night as he'd struggled to fall asleep. He'd bolted out of bed and raced to the window, throwing open the sash as his heart raced. He loved everything about her. He loved her smile, her sense of humor, her compassion. Hell, he loved how she didn't want to make him choose between her and what he wanted out of life. She was amazing. The most considerate person he'd ever met.

And the thing was, he loved her so much, he couldn't make her give up her dreams either. But having to let her go was killing him. Every fiber of his being wanted to hang on tight, to keep her close. A small part of him railed over having to add her to the list of people he'd loved and lost. But at the same time, his conscience berated him for being selfish, reminding him that true love was putting others first. Lisa was doing that, refusing to force him into doing something he didn't want. How could he do anything less for her?

He paced his home, wearing a footpath into the carpets. Everywhere he looked, he noticed something that reminded him of Lisa, of a future with her he couldn't have.

He spun around out of his office and into the living room, filled with family photos. He groaned. Family was what got them into this mess. If only he'd met Lisa when he was younger and at the beginning of his family journey. She wouldn't have left him alone with a baby like Lani had. Instead, she'd have nurtured and adored the child. He could picture Lisa's pleasure raising them. Hell, he could picture the two of them raising a passel of kids together. As partners. Laughing together at the kids' antics, showing a united front when discipline was called for, and glowing with pride over their accomplishments. He swallowed and turned around, trying to wipe away the images of what could have been.

But turning brought his view to the kitchen, and his stomach tightened. If there was one place above all he could picture Lisa, it was here. And not because of some chauvinistic belief that's where women belonged. Nope. Women belonged in whatever space they chose. She adored baking. His mouth watered, recalling all the delicious foods she'd baked. And somehow, remembering her food made him think about her warmth and compassion. He swallowed in frustration. What he needed more than anything was a distraction.

And so, on Monday, he decided to go to his office space downtown to try to get some work done. He owed his clients something tangible for the amount they paid him. Having a home-based business was great. It allowed him the freedom to work however he wanted, whenever he wanted. He wasn't really a work-in-his-pajamas guy, but he liked knowing he could if he *wanted* to. But sometimes, he needed the amenities of an actual office—such as larger meeting spaces and administrative assistants. So he rented a type of hybrid office space in the Emerald Ridge Office Building. And thank God for that. A professional space Lisa hadn't invaded would enable him to concentrate.

He drove downtown, prepared to turn over a new leaf. He wasn't going to tell anyone how hard it had been to force himself out of bed that morning. Nope. He filled his red mug with coffee made by someone else and walked into the office that had not a trace of his personality anywhere. Perfect.

Except, he was wrong. Every plan he looked at reminded him of his gift to Lisa. Every change or adaptation or addition he made caused him to recall her joy when she opened the gift and understood what it was, followed by her tears as she raced from the room. And every time someone came into his office and asked him what was wrong, he realized how bad he was at hiding his feelings.

For their sakes, certainly not his own, he should have stayed home.

The lines and planes he depended on to make sense of life intersected when they weren't supposed to, and didn't when he needed them to, resulting in a jumbled mess that made no sense. He shut his eyes, trying to will his thoughts into something that made sense.

Martin, one of the guys who oversaw the workspace, knocked on Sander's door, entering before Sander had a chance to say a word. *Like I'm busy.*

"The admins are whispering that you're cranky," he said. "They're drawing straws to determine who has to deal with you."

Crap. All he needed was for them to complain loudly enough, and he'd be kicked out. Or worse, get a reputation for being a grump. "I'm not in the mood to joke around," Sander said.

"No, I can see that." He sank into the chair across from his drawing table. "I'm not in the mood to hire new staff though."

Sander had grown to like Martin. He thought Martin liked him too. But as any businessperson would tell you, personal feelings should never get in the way of professionalism. And if Sander couldn't learn to play well with others, he was going to get kicked out of the corral. Deservedly. He ran a hand through his overgrown hair, massaging his scalp in an effort to get rid of the headache coming on. He needed a haircut. "I'm sorry. I'll order them chocolates from Abuela Rose's Chocolates."

Martin flashed a quick grin. "As appealing as that sounds—and if you actually do it, make sure to include something for me, too—I think it would be better if you changed your attitude."

"I'm trying," Sander growled.

"Clearly." He sat back, eyebrow raised, and waited.

He sighed. "You're right, I'm sorry."

"Want to talk about it?"

"A woman I met and fell for, well, we're done." Nausea soured his mouth as the words echoed in the room. Thinking and knowing it were one thing. Saying it out loud to someone was a whole "nuther can o' worms."

"I'm sorry."

"Me too. She wants a family, and I already have one." A family that was grown and self-sufficient.

"There's no meeting in the middle?"

Sander didn't see how. He shrugged.

Slapping the table, Martin pushed out of the chair and headed toward the door, turning at the last minute. "I hope you two can figure out a way through this. I'll try to smooth things over with them," he said, pointing to the admin carrel.

But Sander knew it was hopeless. Loving Lisa wasn't something he'd chosen, and he sure as heck couldn't snap his fingers and make it disappear.

On Tuesday, he sent a huge box of rose tea chocolates to the admins he'd offended yesterday and decided to spare them his presence by attempting to work from home. But, as he suspected, working in his office was useless. Chucking a foam coaster across the room—he'd first reached for his tablet but stopped himself just in time—he left his office, shoving back his chair and rushing outside. He took great gulps of cool air, trying to do something—anything—that would get him back on track. But it was useless. Work wasn't going to happen today.

* * *

He had to find a way to distract himself, to get out of his own head. As he paced the property, willing his lungs to expand enough to take deep breaths, he glanced toward the house. His brother and sister-in-law's bedroom overlooked the backyard. That was it. Instead of work, he'd tackle Mark and Marlene's old bedroom. It had been on his to-do list for weeks, but he'd always found an excuse to push it to the bottom. Today, when he was desperate to think of anything other than Lisa, seemed like the perfect day for the project. Maybe he'd finally find the key to the secret room in the boathouse.

Returning to the house, he raced upstairs and opened the door, pausing to scan the space. Unlike the rest of the house, which had warm wood tones, the bedroom was light and airy, with white-painted wood furniture, colorful quilts and throw pillows, and lots of family photos. When his brother and sister-in-law had first died, he couldn't bring himself to touch this room, much less enter it. But he'd realized their kids needed to be able to enter and remember their parents, so he'd made sure to keep it the way Marlene had decorated it.

The kids had often spent a quiet afternoon reading or doing homework in this room. Once, he'd even stumbled upon Harris napping in here. He still remembered the fear that had gripped him when he hadn't been able to find him, and the relief that had washed over him when he'd entered this room and seen his nephew, his small body tucked beneath the covers. Over time, the acute pain of his brother's loss had lessened, but a heaviness always descended upon him whenever he entered the room, despite the cheeriness of the place. It was a heaviness he tried to hide from the rest of the family.

Inhaling a deep breath and stepping inside the large space, he walked toward the fully made king-size bed. He trailed a hand across the multicolored comforter before he dropped to the floor and looked underneath the bed. He laughed to himself, remembering the countless times he'd done this in one of the kids' rooms. But back then, he'd been checking for monsters.

He'd already done a cursory search of the room, but now he was going to tear everything apart if need be. He snorted. His cleaning lady wasn't going to appreciate the extra mess. He'd have to increase her Christmas bonus. Once again, he thought about Linc's mom, Delia, and how much he missed her. She'd been as much a part of the family as the rest of them, and had been a huge comfort to him when life seemed out of control. Plus, her organizational skills would put the military to shame. If she were here today, she'd help him search. *Scratch that.* If she were here today, he'd bet his ranch that not only would she know exactly where to find the key, but that Linc would still be alive.

Heart heavy, he focused on the problem at hand. He didn't expect to find anything in the space between the floor and the bed. And he was right. But what about within the bed frame? Flattening himself as much as possible, he maneuvered himself beneath the bed and stared at the underside of the mattress through the slats.

A memory from childhood assaulted him—hiding

from his older brother underneath the bed. Mark had been babysitting him, and he'd grown tired of his brother's bossiness, so he'd hidden from him instead of getting ready for bed.

"Jeez, there you are," Mark had said. "I've been looking all over for you. You're such a pain in the neck."

Sander slid out from his hiding place, his glee at outwitting his brother morphing into sadness when he heard Mark's response.

And then Mark grinned. "I'm just teasing. Nice going."

Gosh, he missed his brother.

He ran his hands along the slats. No luck. Climbing out from beneath the bed was even harder—a lot harder than when he'd been a kid—but he managed. Brushing himself off, he opened the drawers of the dresser, checking behind and beneath them as well, before he moved on to the armoire. He opened the closet, filled with old coats and luggage, and checked the pockets. This room had become a catchall for random things no one wanted to clutter up their own homes with, but couldn't bear to throw away. Especially Kelsey, who still hadn't moved all of her things to her new home.

He smiled as he found a stack of old artwork from the kids. At one time, his house had been filled with colorful art projects, toys, and sports equipment. Now it was filled with photos of everyone at different stages of their lives.

Dusting himself off, he righted the mess he'd made

in the closet and scanned the bedroom again. Where the heck could they have hidden the key?

Photos on the wall drew his gaze, and he walked over to a display of Mark and Marlene at various stages in their marriage, and then with their children. Although painful at the time, he had ached to preserve the memories and wanted his nieces and nephews to remember their parents. A wedding photo was centered among photos of the kids. He smiled. He'd been so excited to attend their nuptials and had tried to act older than he was in front of the wedding party. He suspected he'd looked like an idiot, but thankfully, all the groomsmen and bridesmaids had been kind to him that day.

There were more photos on the night table, including one of him and Mark—Mark was much older, probably about twenty, while he had been a baby. He shook his head at what they were wearing—matching cowboy shirts with stitching and bolo ties. Mark had probably hated it, but he'd been a good sport. Either that, or their mother had insisted.

Sander chuffed and picked up the photo. His fingers brushed against something on the back. Turning it over, he groaned. Taped to the back of the frame was a key. *Seriously*? Heart pounding, he stared at it in disbelief. How many times had they searched this room? The cleaning people kept it dusted and vacuumed. The kids had played in here. And none of them found it? Wait until he told everyone...

He pulled the key off the back of the frame and pocketed it. Then, he grabbed his phone and punched in Kelsey's number. He didn't even bother greeting her when she answered. "I found it."

"You found it? Found what?" She gasped. "Oh my God, you found the key? Where was it?"

"You ready for this? Taped to the back of a photo of me and Mark, when I was a baby."

Her gasp echoed through the phone. "No way!"

"Yes, way. I can't believe no one ever found it before now."

"Wait, which photo of the two of you? Where was it?

"In Mark and Marlene's bedroom. The one of the two of us in those stupid cowboy shirts."

She burst out laughing. "All the times I made fun of you in that photo, and *that's* where the key was?"

"Yep."

His daughter groaned. "I can't believe it. The number of times we've seen that photo. How did we miss it?"

He chuckled. His baby girl was voicing everything he'd wondered. "No idea. I'm wondering if there used to be something covering the key at one point and it disappeared over the years? Who knows. Either that or we're completely oblivious. Regardless, maybe now we'll find out if the key opens the locked room in the boathouse."

"When are we going over? Are you going to call everyone? What's next?"

Kelsey's enthusiasm was contagious, but Sander paused. Christmas was only a couple days away and everyone had plans. Besides, not knowing what was hidden in that boathouse, he didn't want to chance upsetting everyone. "I will, but I'd rather wait until after the holidays. No sense bothering everyone now. They've all got Christmas chaos on their minds."

She laughed. "True. I guess we've waited this long. Ugh, although now, knowing how close we are to finally getting some answers…you know I've never been good at waiting."

"Practice makes perfect, kid."

"Speaking of Christmas chaos," she said. "Are you sure you don't want to spend Christmas Day with us?"

Maybe it would be the distraction he needed to get Lisa off his mind. Except, a part of him didn't want to use his family that way. "Even if I did, I don't think I'd be very good company."

"Lisa really got to you, didn't she?" Kelsey asked, her tone growing serious.

He swallowed the lump in his throat. "Yeah. No matter how wrong we might be for each other, I can't stop thinking about her."

"I've never seen anyone affect you the way she does," she pointed out. "Maybe it's a sign you shouldn't ignore." Her sympathy made his chest ache.

"How can I not?" he asked. "Neither one of us wants to hurt the other. You can't build a relationship on that."

"No, but perhaps the issue isn't your different dreams. Maybe it's the person."

He rubbed his eyes, tired of going over the same thing, but unable to give up if he could potentially find a better answer than what he had so far. "What do you mean?"

"Look, you're both being admirable, trying not to

force the other into a dream you don't share. But the truth is, you can't stay away from her. So maybe, for you at least, it's not so much that you don't want another child, but your subconscious recognizes that a relationship with Lisa is going to be different than anything you've experienced in the past." She lowered her voice. "Dad, maybe there's a part of you that realizes she wouldn't leave you to do everything on your own, but that a life with her would be shared, and you'd finally have someone you could depend on."

Sander froze, his body heavy. He sat down in slow motion, as if moving through molasses. It was like the dream where he needed to escape but could never run fast enough. He sank into the chair, his forehead in his hand as he thought about his daughter's words. Could she be right?

"You still there?" Kelsey asked.

"Yeah, I'm here."

"I know how badly you want your freedom, Dad. And if anyone deserves it, it's you. But freedom can be different things to different people. Maybe for you, that freedom is choosing someone who can share everything with you, someone you can depend upon, someone who loves you enough—and who you love enough—to stay."

His throat thickened, and he coughed. "How did you get so smart?"

Was it really that simple? It couldn't be. Could it...?

"I was raised by the best. I love you, Dad." Her voice was soft, and he wished she were here in person so he could give her a hug.

"Love you, too, kiddo."

He sat where he was after she disconnected their call, playing with the idea of raising kids with Lisa. Because he couldn't have her without kids. And if he were honest with himself, the dread he'd felt when he first found out she wanted them had disappeared. On the contrary, thinking of Lisa with a baby—*his baby*—filled him with joy.

He thought back to when Kelsey was a baby, and how overwhelmed and scared he'd been. He remembered the long nights alone, caring for her and his nieces and nephews, the bone-deep panic he'd felt not knowing if what he was doing was right or wrong. If something he did was going to cause long-term damage down the road. He also recalled the frustration of not being able to do something for himself because he had five other humans to think about first. Delia had been around as a sounding board, someone he could depend on for help and advice. Even so, as close as the two of them were, it still wasn't the same bond as he'd have with a wife or partner.

He thought back to his relationship with Lani. Come to think of it, he and Lani hadn't had that closeness either. Pausing, he wondered if he was doomed never to have it. His parents had been close, just like Mark and Marlene had been. So was it him? What had he seen that made him think Lani was a good partner to him? He snorted. If he were honest with himself, he wasn't looking for a partner back then. He's been ruled by other things. But he vowed in the future to be smarter.

Speaking of the future, in Lisa, he saw the possibility of a partnership. A bond they could develop. And suddenly, he wanted that bond with her more than he didn't want children. He paused. Did he really *not* want children? Because if he didn't, it still wouldn't be fair to Lisa, no matter how much he loved her. He paced, running his hand through his hair, his heart beating wildly. How the heck was he supposed to answer that question? Shoot, he shouldn't have hung up with Kelsey so soon. It was weird, needing his daughter for advice, but here he was.

Kelsey. The triplets. Day care.

He phoned his daughter. "Mind if I pick up the triplets for you?"

"Uh, sure, that would actually save me some hassle. But, why?"

He shrugged, unsure of his own reasoning. "Just feel like saying hello."

"I'll call and give them the heads up."

Grabbing his hat, he raced from his house, out to his truck in which he'd installed car seat attachments in the back just in case, and broke every speed limit there was to drive into town. He barely registered the Christmas decorations that festooned the entirety of Emerald Ridge—the huge Christmas tree with bows and lights in the park, the candy canes hanging from the streetlamps, and the shop windows decorated for the season. Screeching to a halt outside the rec center, he turned off the engine and exited his truck. Christmas music piped from outdoor speakers. Around him, everyone stared. Some shook their heads, others opened their mouths as if to say something.

"Sorry," he called as he forced himself to slow his steps. The limestone building faced the park, its frosted windows framed with twinkle lights and bells, its doors covered with wreaths. Entering the lobby, where holiday music played, he strode down the hallway decorated with paper saddles trimmed in white fur, until he reached the play center. The brightly lit room with colorful toys, cheerful teachers and babbling toddlers usually gave him a headache. This time, though, as he looked at the children through the frosted window decorated with snowflakes, his chest filled with love. Flashes of the Grinch with his too-small-heart expanding in size winked in his brain. A little girl had the same red hair as his daughter did when she was young, and he was thrust back twenty years ago to when she was that size. All toothy grins and chubby cheeks and sloppy kisses. His neck ached with the memory of her hugs.

He entered the room and greeted the teachers who were getting his grandkids ready to leave. Reaching down, he picked up James and gave him a hug. An older boy playing with a truck reminded him of Linc when he first arrived, with his big brown eyes, cowlick, and freckles, his complete focus on the task at hand, and a bashful smile when one of the teachers showed him how to attach a ramp to the track. Tears pricked the back of his eyes and he blinked, silently rooting for the kid.

Even the teachers made him think of his nieces and nephews as teenagers. Nodding as they helped him load the car seats in his truck, he couldn't help remembering those first months after his brother and sister-in-law died. They'd had a hard time adjusting to the loss of their parents. Heck, *anyone* would. But they were good kids. Deep down, they were confident and compassionate. While he wasn't the only one responsible for how they'd turned out, he'd certainly helped. Parent-teacher conferences had overwhelmed him, but the teachers had assured him he was doing the right thing. That showing up was half the battle.

Showing up. He'd shown up for everyone who needed him. Maybe it was time for him to show up for someone who wanted him. Because he knew, without a doubt, that Lisa would show up for him.

He signed the form allowing him to leave with the kids. And suddenly, his body ached with a desire to do it all again. To do *this* all over again. As he watched the children playing, his mind filled with images of him and Lisa raising children together. Of the two of them on the floor with however many little ones they had. Her laugh echoing with his over the antics of one of their kids. His gaze boring into hers as they discussed how to handle an issue that arose. Their hands brushing against each other as they reached for diapers together.

Together.

They would do this together.

They *could* do this together.

If she'd still have him.

He gripped the steering wheel as fear coursed through him. His knuckles whitened. Had he lost his chance with her? A sliver of sanity stopped him from racing blindly to her house. If he were going to do this, he couldn't profess his desire to spend the rest of his life with her, to raise children together, if he wasn't positive. An icy sweat ran down the back of his neck. What if he were too late? What if she didn't want him?

She will.

Sander didn't know where that voice came from, but it was louder than his grandchildren fussing in the back seat. The more he thought about it, the more he realized that his happiness lay with Lisa. He'd never depended on another person for happiness before. Heck, he'd never had the opportunity to depend on anyone for anything before. He kind of liked it. Deep breaths in and out calmed him. He still didn't know what would happen next, or how he would feel after this momentary high, but for the first time in a long time, he felt in control. This wasn't something that could be rushed. Because there was no room for error.

Chapter Twelve

"I love Sander, and I'm an idiot," Lisa wailed. Apparently the numbed zombie she'd become after she and Sander parted ways had morphed into an immature teenage girl.

Her mother and sister sat across from her at the kitchen table, a bottle of red wine half empty. They looked at each other, tilted their heads, and turned back to her.

Silence stretched.

Lisa blinked. "Aren't you going to say anything?"

Once again, the two women exchanged glances, before Sara turned to her and said, "And?"

"Isn't that enough?" Lisa's dismay lay in her belly like a heavy matzah ball. She looked from one to the other, waiting for the sympathy they'd always been so good at giving.

But this time, there was none to be found.

Her mother took another sip of her wine. "Honey, announcing you love Sander is like saying the latkes are oily."

Her sister nodded. "You're not saying anything we didn't already know."

Lisa frowned. How could they know what she'd only realized recently? "How is that possible?"

"You wouldn't spend time with a man who didn't want children if your feelings weren't strong," Sara said. "Look at the men you've dated and broken up with because they weren't father material. Yet no matter how much Sander's dream differs from yours, you keep going back to him."

Her mother turned to her sister and leaned toward her ear. "Maybe it's the sex." The whispered words were loud enough for Lisa to hear. Heck, she was tempted to go apologize to her neighbors for the noise.

"Mother!"

"Don't 'mother' me. The man is gorgeous and you're young and healthy."

"It's not the sex," she said, her face heating.

Sara reached for Lisa's wineglass and filled it again. "You look at Sander the way you used to look at Jordan."

The gentleness of her sister's voice made her eyes water. She took a long sip and tried to get herself under control.

"And I've lost both of them," she said.

"Oh, honey." Her mom rose from her seat and came around and hugged her. Her touch made the tears fall.

"God dammit, I swore I wouldn't let myself get hurt like this again," she said after a few moments. "And yet, here I am."

"For the record, I don't think you're an idiot," Sara said. "In fact, I admire your ability to move on."

At one time, the idea of moving on after losing Jordan would have hurt. She'd always love him, but even she could recognize that it was time. If only she'd moved on to someone who was attainable.

"You might admire my ability, but you've got to admit my choice leaves something to be desired."

"Sander Fortune is a kind and generous man," her mother stated. "That's why you fell for him. You'll find someone else, equally kind and generous, who wants children with you." She leaned forward. "Don't give up."

Lisa expelled a shaky breath. "I'm not sure I'm ready to find someone new just yet. It took everything I had to get over Jordan. And I'm not sure I have the energy to find a man and work on the adoption requirements."

Her mom's and her sister's gazes filled with sympathy. "So take a break and focus on the adoption," Sara suggested. "How's that going?"

"My appointment is next week. I'm so nervous. What if they say no?"

"To you?" Her mom scoffed. "Please. There is zero chance of that happening, so worry about something you can control, like the weather." She winked, finally making Lisa laugh.

"Okay, fine." She looked at her watch. "When is everyone else arriving with the Chinese food?"

Her sister checked her phone. "Dad and David and the kids are on their way to pick up the food now. So maybe a half hour? There'll probably be a bit of a line."

Smiling, Lisa played with the stem of her wineglass. "Yeah, the Jewish Christmas Eve tradition." She couldn't stop thinking of Sander. What would he think of her family's tradition? Would he have invited her to celebrate with his family? She shook her head. *I have to stop thinking of what's not meant to be.* But her gaze caught the bright red ribbon on his gift bag, and a lump formed in her throat. She'd never gotten the chance to give him his Christmas gift.

She'd missed a lot of chances with him.

That evening, the family descended on his home ready for their yearly Christmas Eve celebration. Despite his scroogy view of the holiday this year, his chest swelled with love as Roth entered with Antonia and Georgie. Back when they were both young, they'd had a tense history, but thanks to age and time and patience, they'd reached a good place. Sander gave him a tight hug, avoiding his nephew's ever-present Stetson, before kissing Antonia on the cheek and brushing his hand over Georgie's hair.

"Presents in the living room," he said, nodding to the bags in Roth's hands, as right behind them, Priscilla, Jax, and Liam entered. Sander's eyes softened when Liam reached for him, and he took the toddler from Jax's arms as the two adults gave him a hug and went to deposit their gifts.

Sander bounced Liam a bit and made goofy faces, enjoying the squeals of laughter. He could have this again with Lisa…

"Grandpa-hood looks good on you," Harris remarked as his new family arrived.

"It's awesome," Sander said. "Fatherhood looks good on you too," he said quietly. Then in a louder voice, he continued, "Hello, Sofia, hey, Kaitlin, hi, Jackson. Merry Christmas!"

The two kids raced into the living room, while Sofia gave Sander an apologetic look and rushed after the kids.

"You good?" Sander asked Harris.

His nephew's wide grin, as well as the happiness that shone in his green eyes, said it all. Harris slapped his back before the two men followed the crowd into the living room. At the sight of his dad, Liam began to fuss.

That's my cue. Sander handed him over to Jax and turned to greet Trevor, Kelsey, and the triplets. The noise increased, echoing through the open floor plan. But this was Christmas every year, and Sander knew he would have missed it if he'd canceled. He looked around the room at everyone he loved. The only one missing was Zara. He frowned. She hadn't been herself lately either. Regret sat like a lead weight in his chest. He wished he knew how to help her.

Just then, as if thinking about her had conjured her out of thin air, she entered, her long blond hair pulled back in a ponytail, and he walked over to her, enveloping her in a hug. "Can we talk later?" he asked.

She frowned, but nodded, and with that, Sander entered the kitchen to check on the food. The aroma of beef tenderloin marinated in molasses and black pepper made his mouth water, as did the smoked bacon compote. He carried a platter of Indian griddle cakes with corn relish into the living room. Harris's eyes lit up.

"You made them!"

Sander laughed. "Well, not from my own hands, but yes, I'm serving them."

"What about the deviled oysters?" Roth asked.

With a smile, Priscilla left the room, returning momentarily with the favorite dish. "Hurry and take what you all want," she said. "The rest are mine."

Memories of the kids diving for their favorite foods—albeit at the time, their favorites ranged from mac and cheese to chicken nuggets and fries—filled Sander with warmth. He started to understand the joy baking gave Lisa. He wasn't sure if he believed in such things, but if he did, he'd say food was her love language.

Would everything he did today make him think of her?

As much as he loved having his family together for dinners and celebrations, he wasn't a cook, and like every year, he hired someone to cater Christmas Eve dinner. They outdid themselves every time. And, it left him free to see to other important things...although today, it was leaving him lots of time to think about a certain curly-haired brunette.

With the family engaged in chatter, Sander sneaked back into his bedroom, emerging ten minutes later in a Santa suit. A cacophony of sounds greeted him, and he paused in the entryway to the living room, where his daughter, his nieces, nephews, their children and partners congregated. Once again, Lisa entered his head, and he wished she was here, even if it wasn't her holiday. Somehow, he imagined her figuring out the perfect way to fit in. He swallowed, before focusing on bringing joy to the family.

"Ho, ho, ho!" He swooped in and planted a kiss on his daughter's cheek. "Merry Christmas!"

"It's Santa!" Kelsey turned toward the kids. "Look, guys, it's Santa!"

"Santa, Santa, Santa!"

The little ones stared, in some cases grabbing onto their parents as they tried to figure out who this stranger was. But the two older kids, still young enough to believe in Santa Claus, rushed over and gave him a hug. Even through the bulky suit, their bony arms wrapped him in a tight grip, and he patted their backs as love for his family surged through him.

"Merry Christmas! Have you two been good this year?" He deepened his voice, trying to hide anything identifiable about who he might be.

Jackson and Kaitlin looked at each other, as if getting their stories straight, and Sander withheld a laugh. "Yes, we have," they said in unison, faces solemn. He pulled out a LEGO set for the two of them from his sack and watched their glee when they opened it.

"Hey, are you two going to thank Santa?" Sofia asked. She walked up behind them and placed her hands on her children's shoulders.

"Thank you, Santa," they said, before sitting down once again and tearing open the box.

Sander knelt down and focused his attention on the little ones. His heart filled with love as the babies stared at him wide-eyed, until one of the triplet's lips trembled and she burst into tears. A desire to rip off his beard made him clench his hand at his side, but not wanting to ruin it for the others, he ho-ho-ho'd himself across the room to distribute small tokens to Kelsey and his "adult" kids, before moving back to Kaitlin and Jackson and watching their LEGO build.

Christmas music played through the speakers, and his daughter had lit cinnamon-and-clove-scented candles. The tree in the corner of the room was decorated with red-and-white ornaments, and the mantel was covered in fir boughs. Despite his initial desire to avoid Christmas this year, he was glad his family had convinced him otherwise.

As Sander left to change into his street clothes, he looked once more at Kelsey and Trevor. Their union gave him a spark of hope. The two of them were so in tune to each other, and she'd slid easily into the role of mom to triplets. If she could do it, he thought maybe he could too.

Returning to the kitchen, he watched Kelsey and Trevor through the open doorway, feeling their way in their new relationship. And Harris and Sofia as well. They'd all gone through so much and had come out stronger together. Only Zara worried him. As the kids settled down to play with their toys, he walked over to where she stood by the glass door staring outside. He nudged her with his shoulder. She turned, pain in her gaze. His heart ached for her.

"How you doin', kiddo?"

Zara shrugged, and he wrapped his arm around her shoulders.

She stiffened for a minute, before giving in and leaning into him. He stayed silent, hoping she'd talk first.

"I think I'm going to go away for a few days," she said. "To clear my head."

Part of him didn't want her to leave. His Papa Bear raged inside, wanting to keep his niece close and solve all her problems for her. But that wasn't possible, and he knew it. He took a deep breath and kissed the top of her blond head. "I think that's a good idea," he murmured. "When will you leave?"

"Tomorrow morning."

His stomach dropped. He thought she'd just come up with her plan, but clearly, she'd been stewing on it awhile. "Christmas Day? You sure?"

"I am. We're celebrating today as a family. Tomorrow? It's not like I've got anyone to celebrate with."

"You could celebrate with me," he said. "I know how lonely it gets at this time of year."

She wiped her eyes. "I appreciate the thought, but I think I need to get myself together on my own."

He sighed and squeezed her close. He'd been planning to announce that he found the key tonight, but that needed to change. If Zara were leaving tomorrow, he might as well hold off until she returned. They'd waited twenty years, they could wait another week or two.

"I get that. Anything I can do for you?" he asked. He missed the days when they were young and easily helped.

"I don't think so," she said.

Sadness oozed from her voice and his heart ached

for her. He hugged her once more. "Be careful," he said gruffly. "And let me know when you're back safe."

She nodded, before crossing the room. She and Finn were both miserable without each other. He'd seen it in Finn at the stables, and now here, with Zara. But they had to figure out their way—if they had one—on their own.

Clearing his throat, he stepped forward and announced dinner was ready. Everyone made their way into the dining room. The red-cloth-covered table was laden with a warm squab salad with dried-cherry and sorghum syrup dressing, sweet potato confetti, the beef tenderloin and smoked bacon compote, as well as roasted brussels sprouts and corn bread. Wine from the Leonetti Vineyards flowed, and with it, the conversation. As was his tradition, Sander kept the chairs at either end—the ones his brother and sister-in-law had used—empty.

He exhaled, letting the excitement of the moment infuse him. He missed Lisa. He wished she were here with him, but for the first time, he realized how thankful he was for his family. In the past, he'd thought he'd been alone when he'd raised his family. But now he realized they'd stood by him as he navigated his way through premature responsibility and into his recent empty nest.

Sure, as children, they couldn't shoulder the responsibility like he had, but they'd given him their love. And without that, he never would have survived. And now, most of them were busy with their own families, but wasn't that what he wanted for them? He hadn't busted his butt to keep them dependent on him. No, he'd worked his tail off to give them good lives, to make them independent. And they were, for the most part. So that stage of his job was done. For the first time, satisfaction flowed through him as he looked around at the people seated at the table.

They were all successful. Even Zara, though she wasn't quite there, yet.

Now maybe it was his turn. It was time for the next chapter of his life to start.

Chapter Thirteen

Lisa stared at Sander's front door, the large oak double doors with wrought iron hinges and doorknobs foreboding. Gift bag in hand, silent recriminations filling her brain, she wondered why the heck she was here.

She and Sander were done. They'd said so multiple times. She shouldn't be here.

It was Christmas Day, a holiday she didn't celebrate, but he did. Any gift she gave him now would look like she was just doing it to reciprocate. She should return it.

Besides, her gift was nothing compared to what he'd given her. She should stop overthinking, turn around, and just leave.

But she couldn't seem to move off of his front porch.

This was Sander, and she hadn't done anything she *should* do when it came to him from the moment the two of them met. So, despite all the warnings blaring in her head, all the reasons she should turn around and go home, she rang the doorbell and stood her ground, unwilling to play ding-dong-ditch no matter how tempting it might be.

He swung the door wide and her throat dried. Sander

stood in the doorway, leaning on the doorjamb, wearing pajama bottoms and a T-shirt. His sandy hair was mussed, his jaw darkened with an overnight's worth of scruff, and his hazel eyes were bleary.

Until they focused, pinning her in place. Her heartbeat sped up, pattering against her ribs like a prisoner trying to escape.

"Lisa."

Her name on his lips caressed her soul, burned her from the inside out. She blinked, unable to turn away from his laser-like gaze.

She licked her dry lips. "Merry Christmas, Sander." Her hoarse voice grated against her eardrums. She wished she'd practiced speaking in his presence. She wished…for a lot of things.

His gaze dipped to her mouth before once again rising. His hazel eyes pierced her, causing almost physical pain.

This was what happened when she didn't listen to the warnings.

She fought the urge to take a step back.

The corners of his mouth twitched. "You're here."

Her chest ached, knowing *here* was the last place she should be. "I wasn't sure you'd be home today, but I wanted to drop this off for you."

She held out the bag, but he remained still. What was left of her heart pounded, causing a rush of blood to echo in her head. She shouldn't have come. No gift was worth this. All she'd done by showing up on his door was add to his pain, and what kind of person did that to the person they loved? She swallowed. She still loved him, and she was starting to think she always would. But he'd clearly finished with her. He hadn't taken a step forward, hadn't said a word.

Her fingers went cold, and she dropped the bag on the porch before blindly turning around.

"Wait."

The single word from him froze her in place. Her eyes filled with tears, and she tried to blink them away, thankful her back was toward him.

"You don't get to leave me. Not again."

Leave him? Before she could process his meaning, his body pressed against hers from behind, his arms encircled her, and his heat enveloped her.

"I can't let you go again," he whispered, his voice next to her ear. His warm breath made goose bumps rise on her neck and sent shivers down her spine. "Please don't make me."

"Make you?" She swung around in his arms, and he stepped back, giving her the space she wasn't sure she wanted. The broken look on his face told her he didn't want that space either. But his words?

Anger made her tremble. "When have I ever made you do anything? Everything I've done was precisely because I didn't want to 'make' you do something you might regret later." Her breath came in spurts. She wanted to pound him into the ground, make him see how impossibly hard this was for her. Instead, she folded her arms around her waist, gripping the edges of her sweater until she was sure the wrinkled fabric would never lie flat again.

His eyes widened as surprise and regret crossed his features, and he shook his head.

"No, that's not what I meant. I *know* you've never wanted to make me do anything. And it's made me love you even more than I thought possible."

Her mouth dropped. Everything around her froze. Even the clouds seemed to pause in their race across the sky. "You love me?"

She had to have misheard him.

He nodded in slow motion. "More than I've loved anyone. So much, in fact, that the thought of having children no longer scares me, doesn't fill me with dread, but gives me hope."

Her knees trembled, and she reached out her hand to lean against the wood column, red and silver garlands twisting around it. She realized belatedly that her fingers were crushing the decorations, but if she let go, she'd end up on the ground.

"Hope?" Her brain was mush, and all she could do was repeat his words. Nothing made sense.

He nodded. "Yeah. Hope. Hope that we can build a future together, one we share."

It took her a minute to put his words in the right order, for her brain and her heart to come together and understand. And when they did, her chest expanded with joy. Except, she had to be sure. They'd ignored their difficulties too many times, tried to force their square selves into each other's round holes, and had suffered too much for her to take his words at face value. No matter how much her heart longed for what he said to be true.

"I've always wanted a future with you, but I won't make you give up your freedom for me."

"Freedom?" He laughed. "If freedom is this deep loneliness, then I don't want it. I want *you*. I want kids with you. I want a future with you. Forever."

She stepped away from the column with the crushed garland and stared into his warm hazel eyes. "I don't want to force you into doing something you regret later. I *won't* do it."

He cupped her cheek. "Sweetheart, the only regret I'm going to have will be letting you get away."

His palm was so warm against her skin. More than anything, she wanted to turn her head toward it and kiss it. But this had to be a dream. She blinked, sure that when she did, her world would be back to its normal, empty self. But he was still here. Still touching her face, still staring at her. "But you said—"

He took his thumb and pressed it against her mouth. The pressure sent a shiver through her. "I know what I said. But a very wise daughter of mine made me look at things a little differently. And when I finally listened to her, I realized that as long as you and I are together, we can do anything. You're the first person who's ever made me feel like I'm part of something. The only person. Like I can depend on you as much as you can depend on me."

She smiled against his thumb, her body lighter than it had been in a long time. He moved his hand to run it through her hair. "I love you," she said softly. "And more than that, I love the promise of the two of us, together."

He smiled, joy making his eyes glow. "Then let's you and I explore this relationship."

He brushed her mouth with his, and she melted against him, putting all her love, all her desire, into the kiss. And for the first time, her future with this man, this wonderful man, crystallized in her brain.

He pulled back far too soon, reminding her she still had to talk to him about something important.

"I have my appointment with the adoption agency next week."

His eyes lit up. "Can I come?"

If she hadn't already loved this man, she would right now. Pressure built in her chest and she caressed his cheek. "You want to?"

He nodded. "I told you, I'm in this with you. Whatever 'this' is. So if you want to adopt, then let's adopt." He bit his lip. "We should probably get married first though."

Her eyes bugged out. Was he really asking her to marry him?

"Maybe we take things one step at a time? I don't want to rush through anything with you. I want to savor each step."

He wrapped his arms around her. "I feel the same way. So you go to the meeting, but I'll take you there and bring you home, and you can tell me every detail. Deal?"

She nodded, and he kissed her again.

When they finally pulled apart, he spoke. "What did you get me for Christmas?"

She'd practically forgotten her own name, never

mind the gift. She laughed. "A spa day at Fortune's Gold Guest Ranch and Spa. I know it's a little weird, but you always take such good care of everyone around you, I wanted you to be pampered, for once."

He expression softened. "I've never been to the spa before. Thank you. But, honestly, being with you is all the pampering and care I'll ever need."

He lifted her into his arms and carried her into his house, into their future. Together.

* * * * *

*Look for the next installment of the new continuity
The Fortunes of Texas: Fortune's Hidden Treasures*

Fortune's Mr. Right
by USA TODAY *bestselling author Stella Bagwell
On sale January 2026
wherever Harlequin books and ebooks are sold.*

And catch up with the previous books:

His Family Fortune
by New York Times *bestselling author
Elizabeth Bevarly*

Fortune's Fake Marriage Plan
by USA TODAY *bestselling author
Tara Taylor Quinn*

Fortune for a Week
by USA TODAY *bestselling author
Nancy Robards Thompson*

Fortune on His Doorstep
*by Michelle Lindo-Rice
Available now!*

Get up to 4 Free Books!

We'll send you 2 free books from each series you try PLUS a free Mystery Gift.

FREE Value Over **$25**

Both the **Harlequin® Special Edition** and **Harlequin® Heartwarming™** series feature compelling novels filled with stories of love and strength where the bonds of friendship, family and community unite.

YES! Please send me 2 FREE novels from the Harlequin Special Edition or Harlequin Heartwarming series and my FREE Gift (gift is worth about $10 retail). After receiving them, if I don't wish to receive any more books, I can return the shipping statement marked "cancel." If I don't cancel, I will receive 6 brand-new Harlequin Special Edition books every month and be billed just $6.39 each in the U.S. or $7.19 each in Canada, or 4 brand-new Harlequin Heartwarming Larger-Print books every month and be billed just $7.19 each in the U.S. or $7.99 each in Canada, a savings of 20% off the cover price. It's quite a bargain! Shipping and handling is just 50¢ per book in the U.S. and $1.25 per book in Canada.* I understand that accepting the 2 free books and gift places me under no obligation to buy anything. I can always return a shipment and cancel at any time by calling the number below. The free books and gift are mine to keep no matter what I decide.

Choose one:
- ☐ **Harlequin Special Edition** (235/335 BPA G36Y)
- ☐ **Harlequin Heartwarming Larger-Print** (161/361 BPA G36Y)
- ☐ **Or Try Both!** (235/335 & 161/361 BPA G36Z)

Name (please print)

Address   Apt. #

City   State/Province   Zip/Postal Code

Email: Please check this box ☐ if you would like to receive newsletters and promotional emails from Harlequin Enterprises ULC and its affiliates. You can unsubscribe anytime.

Mail to the Harlequin Reader Service:
IN U.S.A.: P.O. Box 1341, Buffalo, NY 14240-8531
IN CANADA: P.O. Box 603, Fort Erie, Ontario L2A 5X3

Want to explore our other series or interested in ebooks? Visit www.ReaderService.com or call 1-800-873-8635.

---

*Terms and prices subject to change without notice. Prices do not include sales taxes, which will be charged (if applicable) based on your state or country of residence. Canadian residents will be charged applicable taxes. Offer not valid in Quebec. This offer is limited to one order per household. Books received may not be as shown. Not valid for current subscribers to the Harlequin Special Edition or Harlequin Heartwarming series. All orders subject to approval. Credit or debit balances in a customer's account(s) may be offset by any other outstanding balance owed by or to the customer. Please allow 4 to 6 weeks for delivery. Offer available while quantities last.

Your Privacy—Your information is being collected by Harlequin Enterprises ULC, operating as Harlequin Reader Service. For a complete summary of the information we collect, how we use this information and to whom it is disclosed, please visit our privacy notice located at https://corporate.harlequin.com/privacy-notice. Notice to California Residents – Under California law, you have specific rights to control and access your data. For more information on these rights and how to exercise them, visit https://corporate.harlequin.com/california-privacy. For additional information for residents of other U.S. states that provide their residents with certain rights with respect to personal data, visit https://corporate.harlequin.com/other-state-residents-privacy-rights/.

HSEHW25